THE MARQUIS IS TRAPPED

The Marquis was aware as they climbed slowly up the stairs that the Earl was somewhat unsteady.

He wondered what had been in the 'night-cap' and was glad he had not touched it.

The lights had already been dimmed to only three sconces in his passage, his own room being in the opposite direction to that of the Earl.

They said goodnight at the top of the stairs and as the Earl was tottering, the Marquis watched him until he reached his bedroom.

Then he walked towards his own room and opened the door.

He turned round to close it and then as he moved a little further into the room he came suddenly to a standstill.

He stared in front of him in sheer astonishment.

His large four-poster bed had a large ornate canopy over it.

Beneath it sitting up against the pillows was Celina!

For a moment the Marquis could not move and was speechless.

Then Celina spoke in a little voice that was hardly audible,

"I am sorry – I am – terribly sorry."

THE BARBARA CARTLAND PINK COLLECTION

Titles in this series

THE MARQUIS IS TRAPPED

BARBARA CARTLAND

Barbaracartland.com Ltd

THE BARBARA CARTLAND PINK COLLECTION

Barbara Cartland was the most prolific bestselling author in the history of the world. She was frequently in the Guinness Book of Records for writing more books in a year than any other living author. In fact her most amazing literary feat was when her publishers asked for more Barbara Cartland romances, she doubled her output from 10 books a year to over 20 books a year, when she was 77.

She went on writing continuously at this rate for 20 years and wrote her last book at the age of 97, thus completing 400 books between the ages of 77 and 97.

Her publishers finally could not keep up with this phenomenal output, so at her death she left 160 unpublished manuscripts, something again that no other author has ever achieved.

Now the exciting news is that these 160 original unpublished Barbara Cartland books are already being published and by Barbaracartland.com exclusively on the internet, as the international web is the best possible way of reaching so many Barbara Cartland readers around the world.

The 160 books are published monthly and will be numbered in sequence.

The series is called the Pink Collection as a tribute to Barbara Cartland whose favourite colour was pink and it became very much her trademark over the years.

The Barbara Cartland Pink Collection is published only on the internet. Log on to www.barbaracartland.com to find out how you can purchase the books monthly as they are published, and take out a subscription that will ensure that all subsequent editions are delivered to you by mail order to your home.

NEW

Barbaracartland.com is proud to announce the publication of ten new Audio Books for the first time as CDs. They are favourite Barbara Cartland stories read by well-known actors and actresses and each story extends to 4 or 5 CDs. The Audio Books are as follows:

The Patient Bridegroom	The Passion and the Flower
A Challenge of Hearts	Little White Doves of Love
A Train to Love	The Prince and the Pekinese
The Unbroken Dream	A King in Love
The Cruel Count	A Sign of Love

More Audio Books will be published in the future and the above titles can be purchased by logging on to the website www.barbaracartland.com or please write to the address below.

If you do not have access to a computer, you can write for information about the Barbara Cartland Pink Collection and the Barbara Cartland Audio Books to the following address:

Barbara Cartland.com Ltd., Camfield Place,
Hatfield, Hertfordshire AL9 6JE, United Kingdom.
Telephone: +44 (0)1707 642629
Fax: +44 (0)1707 663041

THE LATE DAME BARBARA CARTLAND

Barbara Cartland who sadly died in May 2000 at the age of nearly 99 was the world's most famous romantic novelist who wrote 723 books in her lifetime with worldwide sales of over 1 billion copies and her books were translated into 36 different languages.

As well as romantic novels, she wrote historical biographies, 6 autobiographies, theatrical plays, books of advice on life, love, vitamins and cookery. She also found time to be a political speaker and television and radio personality.

She wrote her first book at the age of 21 and this was called *Jigsaw*. It became an immediate bestseller and sold 100,000 copies in hardback and was translated into 6 different languages. She wrote continuously throughout her life, writing bestsellers for an astonishing 76 years. Her books have always been immensely popular in the United States, where in 1976 her current books were at numbers 1 & 2 in the B. Dalton bestsellers list, a feat never achieved before or since by any author.

Barbara Cartland became a legend in her own lifetime and will be best remembered for her wonderful romantic novels, so loved by her millions of readers throughout the world.

Her books will always be treasured for their moral message, her pure and innocent heroines, her good looking and dashing heroes and above all her belief that the power of love is more important than anything else in everyone's life.

"I have always loved the Highlands of Scotland – the soaring peaks of majestic mountains, the misty moorlands, the peace of wild untamed landscapes, the still waters of deep lochs – all inspire my soul and are more romantic than anyone can ever imagine."

Barbara Cartland

CHAPTER ONE
1886

The Marquis of Kexley closed his eyes.

He was feeling incredibly tired, which was hardly surprising considering his lovemaking had been extremely fiery.

Not only that evening, but for the previous nights.

He felt sleepy and yawned,

"It is time I went home. Otherwise when I wake up it will be morning."

"In fact, my dearest Oliver," a soft voice came from beside him, "that would be very much easier and happier for both of us."

For a moment the Marquis did not understand what she was saying.

Then he stiffened.

It had never for one moment entered his head that Lady Heywood would want to marry him.

He thought now that he had been very stupid.

He had not remembered that, as she was a widow, it would be a big step up the Social ladder for her to become a Marchioness.

After being pursued by women from the moment he left his school, the Marquis was only too well aware of his own importance.

He not only held an old and respected title, but he was exceedingly rich.

And, although he tried not to think about it, he was outstandingly handsome.

Now as he felt Isobel Heywood moving closer and still closer to him, every instinct in his body warned him of danger.

"If we were to be married, my dearest," Isobel was whispering so that he could only just hear her, "I know we would be very very happy. You are undoubtedly the most wonderful lover any woman could want and I would make you a dedicated and devoted wife."

The Marquis had to admit that this was true.

Lady Isobel Heywood had taken the Social world by storm when she had first married Lord Heywood, who was nearly thirty years her senior.

He had brought her proudly to Court and naturally the *Beau Monde* had a great deal to say about the stupidity of any man who married a woman young enough to be his daughter.

However, Lord Heywood was infatuated, as a great number of other men were to be in the years to come

His wife was the daughter of a country Squire, who was of local significance, yet not rich enough to give her a Season in London – that would have involved a ball and innumerable luncheon and dinner parties.

All of which would have cost money, and he much preferred to spend his rather meagre income on his horses and the crops on his estate.

Isobel had thus remained somewhat unnoticed in a County where most of the men were near her father's age.

It was by chance that Lord Heywood, when visiting the Lord Lieutenant of Herefordshire, had asked to see the horses of his neighbour.

"I hear he has some outstanding mares," said Lord Heywood, "and I would like to purchase one or two of his as my own mares are getting old."

Isobel's father was suffering badly from an arthritic leg that prevented him from walking far.

So she had therefore taken Lord Heywood around the stables and paddock where the mares were grazing.

Lord Heywood had been a widower for many years as his wife had died in childbirth and he had never had the son he longed for.

By the time he had left Isobel to return to the Lord Lieutenant's house, he had lost his heart.

There was certainly no question of the Squire and his daughter not being thrilled by the offer of marriage – in her wildest dreams Isobel had never thought of herself as marrying a gentleman with a title.

Nor of being feted by the *Beau Monde* that she had read all about in newspapers and magazines.

When she was presented to the Prince of Wales, she thought she must be dreaming.

She became hostess at one of the most impressive houses in Park Lane and she was well aware of the power and attraction of her beauty.

Six years later Lord Heywood had a stroke and died after being unconscious for over three months.

After the funeral Isobel felt she had everything she could ever desire in life and she had only to cast her green eyes in the direction of a man to know that he was entirely captivated.

However, she harboured no intention whatever of marrying again and letting a man gain control of the money her husband had left her.

Yet when she first met the Marquis of Kexley her world turned a somersault.

She then fell in love – definitely something she had never done before.

She realised that what she desired above everything else was to be the Marchioness of Kexley, but she was far too intelligent by this time in her life to rush any fences.

She smiled at the Marquis invitingly, but she did not send him any invitations to dinner or luncheon.

These had to come from *him*.

Eventually he did ask if he could dine with her one evening after they had been seated side by side at a dinner party at Marlborough House with the Prince of Wales.

Isobel hesitated for a second and then she suggested a date at the end of the week.

"Would you like a large party?" she had asked.

"You know perfectly well," the Marquis responded, "that I want to talk to you and to learn a great deal more about you than I know at the moment."

Isobel smiled at him and did not say anything more, as she had achieved just what she desired.

She had bought a new dress for the occasion, which was even more expensive than those she usually wore.

She took a great deal of trouble over choosing the food, and of course, the wine.

When the Marquis arrived at her fashionable house in Mayfair, she thought he might have been a Greek God coming down from Mount Olympus.

She was very aware of the admiration in his eyes as she moved towards him glittering with diamonds.

Her exquisite figure was displayed by the tightness of her gown and the smallness of her waist.

The Marquis was expecting a large party, but was not all that surprised to find that he was the only guest.

Every word over dinner had a *double entendre*.

They went into the drawing room when dinner was finished, but they were both so well aware that it would be much pleasanter and more comfortable to move down the passage towards the State Apartments.

When they met again three nights later there was no question of going first to the drawing room.

At the age of thirty Isobel was at the height of her great beauty and charm and she was extremely experienced where men were concerned.

She had been faithful to her elderly husband for more than two years, but after that whenever he was sent on Government missions abroad or to the country whilst she remained in London, she took a lover.

With her beauty and her husband's position, it was very easy.

There were always gentlemen eager to make love to a new beauty, who was admired by every member of their Club in St. James's Street.

Where Isobel was concerned, it made them feel as proud as if they had just won the Gold Cup at Ascot – or, as one admirer told her, his horse had been first past the winning post in the Derby!

Whilst Isobel enjoyed the admiration and attention she received from her many lovers, they were not of any real significance to her.

Only when she met the Marquis did her heart begin to rule her head.

She definitely wanted to be a Marchioness and at the same time she wanted to possess his heart and body.

Now as she snuggled closer to him, she thought he must feel the same as she did.

After what she had just said, he would tell her they would find eternal happiness together as man and wife.

Instead, to her great surprise, she suddenly realised that he was asleep – his eyes were closed and he seemed to be breathing evenly.

He had obviously not heard a word of what she had just said to him!

Another woman might have been stupid enough to wake him up and repeat her suggestion.

But Isobel was too clever for that.

'I will ask him again tomorrow,' she told herself.

Then she laid her head gently onto his shoulder.

It was several minutes before he awoke with a jerk and for a moment he seemed to look round the room as if he was not certain where he was.

Then he exclaimed,

"Forgive me – I fell asleep! I can only apologise."

"You are tired, my dearest, and it is not surprising!"

"How could I be so foolish as to sleep when I am so close to you?" the Marquis asked, shaking his head.

Then he turned towards her and added,

"I must go home. Otherwise we shall be woken up by your lady's maid who will be extremely shocked to find you are not alone."

"There is no hurry," cooed Isobel softly.

"I have to think of your reputation."

The Marquis kissed her cheek and then quickly got out of bed.

Too late she put out her arms to stop him.

"It must be nearly four o'clock," he remarked as he began to dress. "And now I think of it, I have an important engagement this morning. I must hurry home and snatch some rest or I will not make any sense at all."

"You do know that I want you to stay with me," she murmured softly. "I shall be *very* lonely without you."

"I can only thank you for an entrancing evening – "

"When can we dine together again? Tomorrow, or rather tonight?"

The Marquis shook his head.

"I have a feeling I have accepted an invitation from Marlborough House. I will let you know in the morning."

He was dressing with a swiftness and expertise that always annoyed his valet.

He had learnt to tie his tie better than anyone could tie it for him and he smoothed his hair back in front of the mirror.

It would have been difficult for anyone to guess at what he had been doing for the last three hours.

He turned from the ornate dressing table to Isobel who was watching him closely.

She was lying back languidly against lace-trimmed pillows with her dark hair falling over her white shoulders in a most alluring manner.

As the Marquis walked towards her, she held out both her arms.

"Kiss me good morning, my darling," she begged.

The Marquis smiled at her.

Then taking one of her hands in his, he raised it to his lips.

"I have been caught in that trap before," he joked.

If a man allowed a woman to place her arms round

his neck when she was lying below him, he would topple over her.

And then it would be difficult to escape.

Isobel's fingers closed over his.

"You will not forget me, darling Oliver?"

"That is seriously impossible."

"Do stay just a little longer," she implored. "I have something of importance to say to you."

"You are not to tempt me, Isobel, as otherwise my business meeting this morning will be a farce."

He moved away to the door before she could reply.

As he pulled it open, she gave a little cry.

"Oliver! Oliver! I cannot let you go!"

He smiled benignly at her.

Then without another word he went out of the room closing the door gently behind him.

She could hear his footsteps going quietly along the passage as she bent forward to listen.

Then she threw herself back against the pillows.

'I will ask him again,' she decided, 'the next time he comes. I should have suggested it before he became so sleepy. It was stupid of me.'

She was almost angry with herself.

Then, sitting up in bed, she pulled on the soft chiffon nightgown that had been lying on the foot of her bed.

*

The Marquis walked briskly up Park Lane feeling the morning breeze on his face.

The stars overhead were disappearing and in a short time the first rays of dawn would be creeping into the sky.

He walked with determination.

He felt somehow it was absolutely essential for him to distance himself from Isobel as soon as possible.

How on earth, he asked himself, could he have been so foolish?

How had he not anticipated that sooner or later she would want to marry him as so many other women had?

For them it had been impossible as they already had a husband.

He had recognised by the time he was twenty that it was most dangerous for him to have anything to do with *debutantes*.

His father had warned him in the first place and he had already seen several of his contemporaries caught by ambitious mothers and hurried up the aisle well before they could realise what was happening.

The Season in London, amusing and attractive as it could be, was extremely dangerous for a young man who had either a title or a fortune.

Every aspiring mother was determined that by the end of the London Season her daughter should be engaged to be married.

Or that she should have received so many proposals that any man accepting as a suitor would feel he had won a difficult battle.

There were, however, fortunately for men just like himself, who had no wish to be married off, a great many restrictions.

No well brought up young girl was ever allowed to be left alone with a man even for half-an-hour in a drawing room.

All women of every age expected men, the instant they found themselves alone with one, to flirt and admire them.

The Marquis was exceedingly intelligent, and as soon as he left University his father had sent him round the world.

Thus he automatically sought much more mature conversation than he was likely to enjoy with a *debutante*.

Most *debutantes* had been educated by a Governess who did not know much more than the girl knew herself.

When he was resident in London the Marquis found married women to be exciting as well as amusing.

Their husbands neglected them for sport or for their duties at Windsor Castle as the Queen was very demanding and liked men round her who were bright and interesting.

This then meant that a great number of beautiful and experienced ladies in Society spent much of their time alone either in their London or country houses.

It was, of course, as the Marquis soon found, very much easier when they were in London.

There would usually be a formal dinner party with a few elderly guests who left early. When they had gone, if one man stayed behind, there was no one left to count the hours of how long he lingered.

The women that intrigued the Marquis were usually a little older than himself.

They were always amusing and inevitably beautiful and well aware of their own attraction.

The Marquis actually had more to offer than most of the other younger gentlemen in the Social world.

He had therefore passed from boudoir to boudoir gaining a great deal of most enjoyable experience.

But above all he became determined that he himself would not marry until he was very much older.

Although he would never admit it, he was deeply shocked that all the women he made love to should be so blatantly unfaithful to their husbands.

It was always quite obvious that he was not the first beau who had eaten their husband's food, drunk his wine and slept in his bed.

At the back of his mind the Marquis became more and more aware that this was something he would never tolerate in his own wife.

At the same time it was quite impossible to resist the invitation in a pair of lovely eyes, or the soft movement of two red lips that told him what he wanted to hear.

With all his experience in London, Isobel had been his first widow.

Now, as he was walking home, he realised how by only a hair's breadth he had managed to escape the trap she had set for him.

As he looked back over his *affaire-de-coeur* with Isobel he was sure that she had intended to marry him from the very first moment they had met.

Now he could fully appreciate the little things she had said that had seemed of no importance at the time.

If he had been intelligent, he would have read the warning signs.

'How can I have been such an idiot?' the Marquis asked himself again as he turned into Grosvenor Square.

His house, which had been in the family since the Square was first built, was the largest and most fashionable in Mayfair.

He knocked on his front door and the night footman hurried to open it for him.

The Marquis now walked into the hall that was lit by only two candles on the marble mantelpiece.

"Any messages for me, Henry?"

"Only some letters, my Lord."

They were lying on a table and the Marquis looked at them.

"They can wait for Mr. Foster in the morning."

"I'll put them on his desk, my Lord."

The Marquis walked up the stairs.

As usual he had ordered his valet not to wait up for him, but everything was ready for him in his room.

He undressed, but instead of getting into his bed, he walked to the window and pulled back the curtains.

Now the first rays of light were flickering over the roof and the last evening star was fading with the darkness. There was the soft hush in the air that always comes before the dawn.

The Marquis was thinking only of himself and the soft voice of Isobel suggesting that they should be married.

The idea horrified him.

How could he possibly marry any woman he could not trust and who would be unfaithful to him the moment he left home?

He had always hated the idea of being tied down – of taking a wife as was expected of him because it was so important he should produce a successor and heir.

He felt as if marriage would imprison him.

It would take away his freedom, which, although he had not thought of it often, was very precious.

He had seen so many of his dear friends captured and compelled to live a life that was entirely different from anything they really enjoyed.

The longer he had participated in the Social world, the more he considered that its rules and regulations were ridiculous.

Debutantes and all young girls, he had found, were

treated as if they were treasures and they went nowhere without a chaperone.

Nevertheless, if they managed to sit out too long with a young man at a dance, the parents could accuse him of ruining her reputation and then he would be obliged to offer her marriage.

If anyone danced two consecutive waltzes together, every chaperone in the room would start whispering loudly and excitedly to those sitting nearby!

Such a daring procedure spelt out the stirring word – '*bethrothed*.'

The Marquis had soon become conscious that every ambitious mother was after him as a matrimonial catch.

He received innumerable invitations from hostesses he had never met for balls, dinner parties and *soirées* of every description.

His secretary had learnt to refuse them on sight, but they still came piling into the letter box day after day.

When the Marquis attended a ball, which was often, he took great care to dance only with married women.

Wearing their tiaras they smiled at him invitingly as soon as he arrived in the ballroom.

It was their invitations he accepted, despite those which came regularly to him from Marlborough House.

The Prince of Wales liked young gentlemen who were handsome and influential.

He himself had set the fashion for the first time for a gentleman to have an *affaire-de-coeur* openly with a lady of his own class.

'The Jersey Lily' as she was called, had opened new paths in the Social world that had always been sealed in the past. Once Princess Alexandra had accepted Mrs. Langtry, it was quite impossible for anyone else in Society to ignore her.

It made things, the Marquis considered, very much easier in some ways, but it certainly meant that the husband in question was always made to look a complete fool.

'I will *not* allow that to happen to me,' the Marquis determined.

Then he wondered if he would be able to prevent it.

Unless a man married a woman so unattractive that no one else would waste any time on her, it was impossible to ensure that when he was away from home someone else was not taking his place at his table and in his bed.

On his twenty-sixth birthday the Marquis had given a party at his ancestral home in the country, Kexley Place, and a great number of his relatives had come to stay.

Almost all of them had asked him at some time or another when he intended to be married.

He had refused to argue about it, merely saying,

"When it suits me, and that will not be for a very long time."

"But, Oliver," they protested, "you have to have a son. Do you realise the Marquisate will end completely if you do not produce an heir?"

"I wonder if that will matter one way or another," he had replied provocatively.

He had then received loud screeches of horror from every relative to whom he said it.

When he visited London, he had thought he would feel uncomfortable at taking another man's place where his wife was concerned.

But somehow it was impossible not to be attracted by an invitation in two intriguing eyes.

He found himself again and again walking home at the break of dawn having enjoyed yet another rapturous encounter with a beauty whose husband was conveniently away in the country.

'It is wrong! It is wrong!' the Marquis had said to himself on countless ocasions.

At the same time he knew he would be lonely if he went home early to an empty house.

The best alternative was someone sweet, warm and gentle nestling against his body, telling him endlessly how much she loved him.

It was clearly something no man had the strength to refuse.

Now, as the Marquis walked upstairs, he was faced with a different problem that he knew could be dynamite in Isobel's hands.

He thought again how foolish he had been not to realise that Isobel harboured a genuine affection for him as well as being exceedingly ambitious Socially.

He had not really considered it of any particular importance, but he was now aware that she wanted a more significant title than the one her husband had given her.

He had fully recognised, although it did not really concern him, that she was irritated when Duchesses and Countesses took precedence to her at dinner parties.

She was seldom seated on the right of the host, and looking back the Marquis could remember little incidents when a lady with a superior title would sweep past her or even spoke to her in a condescending manner.

It was all part of the Social game, which he thought was somewhat laughable and in many ways quite idiotic.

Yet to a woman it mattered – and he knew now that it mattered to Isobel.

If she was married to him, she would ascend a great number of steps higher on the Social ladder.

Now he was confronted with the vexed question as to whether he would marry her or not.

The Marquis was startled by his own feeling almost of revulsion at the thought.

If he ever married, it would not be to a woman who would be unfaithful to him, nor one who wanted him more for his title and his money than for himself.

Yet, he asked, was it possible there was any woman in the world to whom these two things did not matter?"

And anyway he was very determined to marry only when he was really in love.

'I suppose,' he pressed on in his mind, 'I am just expecting too much of life as it is lived in this dimension, or should one say in the *Beau Monde*. Women want Social status and money. They know the more beautiful they are, the more they are likely to achieve it.'

Then, almost fiercely, as if he felt threatened, the Marquis vowed,

'But not where *I* am concerned!'

He turned towards the window and pulled back the curtain sharply as if he was slamming a door, and then he climbed into bed and blew out the candles.

Although he was tired, he did not fall asleep.

Instead he was wondering what he should do about Isobel. He was certainly used to the curtain coming down on his love affairs unexpectedly.

How was he going to tell her that their *affaire-de-coeur* was at an end?

At this moment he had no wish to see her again and most of all he did not wish to even discuss, as he knew she would insist, whether or not they should be married.

It would be embarrassing for him and also he was

not certain as to how she would take the idea of their affair closing down so abruptly.

Some women he left had wept copious tears.

Some had written pleading letters.

Just one or two had accepted the silence between them as something that could not be altered and made no comment of any sort.

Later in the morning, his secretary, as was usual in such situations, would despatch a large bouquet of orchids or roses to Isobel.

There would be no card or letter with it, because it was the Marquis's sense of protection not to put anything in writing.

He had never written love letters as he knew how dangerous they could be if a husband became suspicious about his wife's behaviour.

Isobel would receive her orchids, but she would not be aware that they marked the end of an affair that she had hoped would end in marriage.

Still she would be expecting him for dinner.

If not tonight, then the night after or the night after that.

But what would come after that? If she did not hear directly from him, she would then undoubtedly demand an explanation.

'I have to do something,' the Marquis reflected.

Then an idea came to him.

Foster had told him just casually yesterday morning when he was writing his letters that the alterations ordered for his yacht had been completed.

"As the Captain thought your Lordship would like to see them," Mr. Foster had continued, "he is bringing *The*

Neptune up the River Thames and will moor it just above Westminster Bridge."

The Marquis had nodded and then he had continued dictating a letter about some other issue.

Now he remembered that his yacht would be close by and the Captain would be waiting for his inspection.

'Perhaps I will sail away,' he pondered and then he wondered where he should go.

Almost as if he was being prompted he recalled that amongst his correspondence yesterday morning was a letter that he had not expected.

It was from an old friend of his father's, the Earl of Darendell, who had written to him from Scotland saying,

"Dear Kexley,

"I have seen your name mentioned a few times in the Social columns of the newspapers and realise that you have been back in England for some time.

As you will doubtless remember, I was a very close friend of your father's for many years, and I am wondering if you would like to come to Scotland at any time and stay with me at Darendell Castle.

Our river at the moment seems to be full of salmon, and your father was a very fine fisherman.

My wife and I would welcome you at any time this month or next and it would be delightful to talk of the old days and how much I have enjoyed staying in your house in Berkshire.

Yours very sincerely
Darendell."

The Marquis had been touched by the letter.

He remembered the Earl as a most interesting and intelligent man and he had been one of his father's oldest friends and they had been at school together.

He had never been to Darendell Castle in Scotland, but he had heard a great deal about it.

It now struck him that this invitation could almost be an answer from Heaven.

It was where he should go to escape from Isobel.

If he left immediately, it would save the arguments, accusations and inevitable tears.

He would also not feel uncomfortable every time he saw her at Marlborough House or at any other party.

'It will be running away,' he told himself, 'but there is nothing else I can do.'

Then he lent back against his pillows.

It was a long time since he had fished for salmon and it was a sport he had always enjoyed with his father.

Strangely enough he had not been to Scotland since he had grown up although he had been there twice while he was still at Eton and each time he had stayed with friends in Edinburgh.

Now he ruminated about it, Darendell Castle was much further up the East coast of Scotland – unless he was mistaken, it was in Sutherland.

'It is something I might well enjoy,' he wondered.

He remembered that the Earl was an elderly man and any other guests staying in the Castle would doubtless be his contemporaries as his father had been.

Therefore he would be safe from women pursuing him and attempting to trap him into marriage.

Once again he felt that he could hear Isobel's voice so soft, gentle and beguiling, suggesting quietly that they should be married.

It would just be impossible for him to tell a woman, especially one as beautiful as Isobel that he did not love her enough for that particular sacrifice – nor that he considered her behaviour was something he would ever tolerate in his own wife.

She would be furious with him and would doubtless make him a laughing stock.

There would be quite a large number of Socialites who unfortunately would be only too pleased to say that he had behaved badly and perpetuate endless scurrilous gossip about him.

In a way the situation was ironic.

It was accepted that he could not marry the women he had made love to if they were already married, while it would be considered very wrong and ungentlemanly if he refused to marry one of them who wished to marry him and was free to do so.

'It is all too complicated and incomprehensible for me,' the Marquis decided.

He might indeed be deemed a coward to run away, but he had no wish to stay and face the music.

'The quicker that I leave London the better.'

Then having made the decision, the Marquis turned over and closed his eyes.

As he did so, he could almost hear Isobel pleading with him and at the same time exciting him as she was able to do so successfully.

'And with a great deal of experience,' he thought cynically.

'I shall be going away,' he determined firmly, 'and I will find some excuse for leaving. Nothing and no one will prevent me from doing what I want to do – '

And the final words of that sentence were,

'To remain unmarried.'

Then again he could hear all his relatives pleading with him to produce an heir.

And Isobel repeating to him so softly, seductively and irresistibly how blissfully happy they would both be if she was his wife.

"*Never!* Never! Never!" the Marquis shouted out loud.

His voice seemed to ring out in the darkness of his bedroom.

CHAPTER TWO

The Marquis woke as his valet was pulling back the curtains.

He had slept deeply and dreamlessly.

It took a little time to remember that he had a busy day ahead of him.

Gilbert, his valet, came to his side.

"It's nine o'clock, my Lord."

The Marquis stared at him in surprise.

"Nine o'clock!" he exclaimed. "Why have I been called so late?"

"I did look in earlier, my Lord, but your Lordship were fast asleep. As you was late coming in and have no engagements for this morning, I thinks it'd do you good to rest for a bit."

The Marquis smiled where another man might have raged.

Gilbert had been with him ever since he left Oxford and had travelled with him around the world. He always seemed to behave rather like a nanny who was determined not to let her charge get into any trouble.

What he had done for him this morning was out of sheer affection and the Marquis could never scold him for that.

He pulled back the bedclothes.

"I must get up at once," he said, "because actually,

although you were not aware of it, I have a great deal to do. We will be leaving for Scotland later this afternoon in the yacht."

"Scotland, my Lord. That be something new."

The Marquis laughed.

"I think it is something really I do need and that is why we are going there."

As he walked towards his bathroom, he turned back to order,

"Send now for Captain Gordon, Gilbert. My yacht is moored just above Westminster Bridge."

Gilbert hurried away to obey his command.

The message was then relayed to the mews to send a conveyance to *The Neptune*.

It did not take the Marquis long to bathe and dress and he walked slowly downstairs for his breakfast.

There was a whole row of silver entrée dishes on the sideboard waiting for him.

Enough, the Marquis had often thought, for a dozen rather than just one, but it would have insulted the cook, who also had been with him for a great number of years, if he had complained in any way about the food or the large array of dishes.

When he had finished his breakfast, he went to the study.

He had always thought that it was one of the most attractive rooms in the house. His father had made it very picturesque and it looked out onto a garden at the back.

It contained some of the best sporting pictures in the Marquis's collection.

As soon as he was seated at his desk his secretary, Mr. Foster, came hurrying in.

"You have not forgotten, my Lord," he asked, "that you are having luncheon with His Royal Highness today?"

The Marquis knew by his agitated manner that Mr. Foster had already been told, perhaps by Gilbert, that he was leaving for Scotland.

"I have not forgotten, Foster. I will go straight from Marlborough House to the yacht. See that I am supplied with everything I might need for the voyage, and of course, that includes some of the best champagne."

"The arrangements are in hand, my Lord, but your Lordship will have to refuse so many invitations that you have already accepted."

"I know, but my excuse is that an old friend of my father's has been taken ill and has asked me to come and see him. I have to leave at once, as his doctors fear he has only a short time to live."

"I understand, my Lord, and, of course, I offer you my commiserations."

The Marquis did not explain to Mr. Foster that what he had said was factitious, as he had merely decided that it would be the same explanation he would give to Isobel for his absence.

Mr. Foster had a great number of letters for him to sign and bills to be paid.

When all this was finished, he gave Mr. Foster the address of where he would be staying.

Then the butler announced that Captain Gordon had arrived from *The Neptune* and the Marquis felt pleased that his instructions had been carried out so quickly.

Mr. Foster left and the Captain was shown in.

It was usual to call a naval Officer commanding a private yacht, 'Captain', although John Gordon had been in the Royal Navy and had not served long enough to reach the rank of Captain in Her Majesty's fleet.

After the Marquis had engaged him, he realised he had been very fortunate.

He was employing an excellent Captain, who was not only experienced but had a real love of the sea and he was very enthusiastic when it came to improving the yacht. The crew he engaged were nearly all ex-naval men.

The Marquis rose and held out his hand to welcome the Captain.

"It is good to see you, Gordon, and I hope that all my new ideas have been put into practice."

"They have indeed, my Lord," replied the Captain, "and I am pleased to have the chance of speaking to you so soon after leaving the shipyard."

"You have moored *The Neptune* near Westminster Bridge?"

"It is where we have been before, my Lord, and we have an excellent berth with no problems."

"Well, you will not be staying there long, as we are leaving this afternoon for Scotland."

The Captain looked at him in surprise.

"For Scotland!" he exclaimed.

"I thought you would be pleased at the idea as you are a Scot yourself, Gordon, and we are going to the very far North. In fact to Darendell Castle, which I am sure you have heard about."

"I have indeed, my Lord, but it takes me rather by surprise since, having completed the work you required on the yacht, I was going to request your permission for a few days holiday."

The Captain thought that the Marquis stiffened and he went on quickly,

"I have not had any chance to inform your Lordship before, but I was married last week to someone I have been very fond of for many years."

"Married! That is a bit of a surprise."

"I wanted to marry her – she is also a Scot – some years ago, but unfortunately she had an ailing mother, who she has had to wait on hand and foot. It was impossible to leave her, but she was not really ill enough to be accepted in a hospital."

"I understand – and I suppose she has now died?"

"She has indeed died and it was a merciful release for everyone, especially her daughter. So we were married last week in the village Church and I can only say to your Lordship that I am a very fortunate and happy man."

"Of course, you have my congratulations, Gordon, but as I am very anxious to leave for Scotland immediately, would it be possible for Mrs. Gordon to accompany you on *The Neptune*?"

The Captain stared at the Marquis in astonishment.

"I will be travelling alone, and it would therefore be possible for you and your bride to occupy one of the larger cabins than you would normally use. I just cannot believe that, as a Scot married to a naval Officer, Mrs. Gordon will not enjoy the sea as much as we will."

"But, of course, she will! It's exceedingly generous of your Lordship to suggest something that would make our honeymoon very much more glamorous than anything I could offer or afford."

The Marquis laughed and spread out his hands.

"*The Neptune* is at your disposal, and I assure you, Captain, that I will not intrude on your honeymoon."

"It's just the sort of kindness, my Lord, that I might have expected from you. As you are giving me and my wife a honeymoon we will always remember, I'll strive to make the voyage as comfortable and pleasant as I possibly can for your Lordship."

"You must tell me, Gordon, what you would like in the way of a wedding present, although it may have to wait until we return."

The Captain thanked him again profusely and then he left hurriedly to make preparations for the voyage and to collect his bride, who fortunately was staying not far from where the yacht was moored.

The Marquis rang the bell for Mr. Foster.

"As we have a bridal couple aboard," he said, "the least we can provide is a wedding cake and champagne."

"I have never seen a man more pleased, my Lord, at setting off on a voyage as the Captain was when he left just now, and as I have not heard before about his marriage, it took me by surprise."

"I have often wondered just why the Captain was a bachelor, and I thought that perhaps like me he wanted to be free."

"From what he told me as he was leaving, my Lord, he has waited for years for this particular woman and is jumping over the moon now he actually possesses her."

The Marquis did not say so, but he felt that this was the real love that all men always sought in their dreams but very few found.

He could not imagine himself waiting for years for any of the women he had made love to – then even to think of them brought back the menace of Isobel!

The sooner he was out of her reach the better.

The Marquis was thinking that it was time he drove to Marlborough House when the door of the study opened suddenly and the butler announced,

"Lady Heywood, my Lord."

Isobel had called at the house a number of times on one pretext or another.

Therefore she was not shown, as would have been usual, into one of the reception rooms, whilst the Marquis was informed of her arrival.

As she now flounced into the study, he rose from the writing table.

He knew he had to be very astute if he was to avoid a scene.

"This is a surprise, Isobel!" he called as she walked towards him.

He had to admit that she was looking exceedingly beautiful.

She was wearing a pink gown and a hat trimmed with pink feathers. They were a perfect background for her dark hair and her sea-green eyes.

As the door shut behind her Isobel ran towards him.

"I felt I had to see you," she said, putting her hands on his shoulders.

She looked up at him.

The Marquis saw by the expression in her eyes that she was even more dangerous than he had anticipated.

"This is such a surprise, Isobel," he repeated. "But as I have told you before, it is a great mistake for you to call here when there is no one staying with me."

"What does it matter what people say?" she asked. "It would be quite easy, my dearest Oliver, to prevent them saying anything, if – "

The Marquis was aware that she was about to say the words he dreaded.

Before they could actually pass her lips he bent his head and kissed her.

For the moment she was unable to speak and then he raised his head and remarked quickly,

"I am about to leave for Marlborough House and I must not be late – it always annoys His Royal Highness."

"I know, my darling," replied Isobel. "But I have something *so* important to discuss with you and I promise you it will not take long."

The Marquis realised what she was about to say.

He looked at the clock on the mantelpiece.

"I must go!" he cried. "His Royal Highness wishes to have a word with me before luncheon and I am already late. Forgive me, dearest, but I cannot stop any longer."

He moved sharply away from her clinging hands to walk towards the door.

"But Oliver I must see you, I *must*!"

"Tonight, I will be with you at seven o'clock."

The Marquis did not wait for an answer, but ran out of the study and into the hall.

To his considerable relief, he could see through the open door that his carriage was waiting outside.

He knew that Isobel would be following him, so he snatched his top hat from one footman and his gloves and stick from another.

Then before she could reach the hall he had stepped into his open carriage and a footman closed the door.

The horses began to move forward and as he drove away, the Marquis looked back.

He could see Isobel standing just a little way from the butler with an expression of anxiety on her face.

The horses turned out of Grosvenor Square and the Marquis gave a sigh of relief.

He had escaped – for the time being.

He could only hope and trust that Isobel would not find out from his servants that he was leaving for Scotland that afternoon.

If she learnt the truth and that he was going there in his yacht, she would undoubtedly find her own way there by some means or other.

Then he reassured himself that Bolton, his butler, who had been with him for many years, knew that he must never under any circumstances impart information about his Master's movements without his permission.

If Isobel asked any questions, he was sure that she would receive answers that would give her no knowledge of what he was doing.

Once he was at sea, it would be impossible for her to follow him.

The Marquis reckoned, as the carriage drove down Piccadilly, that he had had a very narrow escape.

But he was not yet completely out of the woods.

Once again he was asking himself how on earth he could have been so foolish or so blind.

Why had he not suspected Isobel's intentions from the very first moment he made love to her?

'I will have to be extremely careful in the future,' the Marquis vowed.

From now onwards widows as well as *debutantes* were definitely taboo.

He arrived at Marlborough House just a little earlier than the other guests and the door was smartly opened by a Scottish ghillie in Highland dress who knew him.

"Good day, my Lord," he welcomed him in a strong accent, "it's good to see your Lordship again."

A powdered footman in a bright scarlet coat took the Marquis's hat and a page in a dark blue coat and black trousers then led the Marquis up to the first floor.

The Prince of Wales was waiting for him in a room panelled in walnut with tall windows overlooking Pall Mall and greeted him warmly.

"I have been wanting to have a word with you for some time, Oliver, but we always seem to be surrounded by beautiful women who demand our full attention!"

The Marquis did not answer and after a moment the Prince gave him a sharp look.

Then he enquired,

"I don't wish to be impertinent, but are you happy? Isobel Heywood told me the last time she dined here how much she loved you and begged me to help her."

The Marquis thought this was quite a familiar move by many women, as they were well aware that the Prince of Wales always wanted to be told a secret before anyone else – whether it concerned love, marriage or a question of money and he liked his friends to ask for his assistance.

This was, the Marquis realised, the result of being treated so badly by his mother, the Queen, who deliberately excluded him from any of the decisions that concerned the Government or the Empire.

He was not even permitted to scrutinise the reports submitted by the Foreign Office, although he had been a great success on his visits to France and to other countries in Europe.

The Prince was frustrated because he was given no position except that of Heir to the Throne.

It was therefore not surprising that he spent his time chasing and possessing beautiful women and had therefore gained the reputation of being a *roué*.

Because the Marquis knew it would please him, he replied,

"I have been hoping for a chance, sir, of confiding in you, because I am in a *most* difficult position."

The Prince of Wales was immediately alert.

"In what way, Oliver?"

"I suspect," he murmured choosing his words most carefully, "that Isobel Heywood wishes to marry me."

The Prince raised his eyebrows.

"*Marry you!*" he exclaimed. "I had not thought of that. I know that she is in love with you, because she told me so."

"I find her very attractive," the Marquis conceded. "But, as Your Royal Highness knows, I have no wish to be married. In fact I have a *horror* of it!"

The Prince gave a little laugh.

"That is not surprising. But you are too handsome, too rich and too grand, my dear Oliver, for any woman not to think you are the ripest plum she could pick off a tree!"

"I am indeed flattered and honoured. At the same time I have no intention of 'settling down,' as my relatives call it, and marrying some woman I have no wish to spend the rest of my life with, simply so that she can present me with an heir."

"I understand, my dear boy, exactly what you are saying, but you will have to marry sooner or later."

"*Later* is the better word, sir, and, as I am not yet twenty-seven, there is still plenty of time."

"Of course, of course," the Prince agreed. "But I see that at the moment your problem is Isobel Heywood."

The Marquis drew in his breath.

"I have so far been able to prevent Isobel, sir, from actually asking me to place a ring on her finger. But it is only a question of time before I have to declare myself one way or another, and as Your Royal Highness will be aware, it will be extraordinarily difficult."

"Of course it will," the Prince said sympathetically. "Now let me think."

He put his hands up to his face.

As he did so, the Marquis remarked,

"I thought as my yacht has been newly renovated, I might pay a visit to Scotland."

"An excellent idea!" the Prince exclaimed. "I was in fact going to suggest something of the sort myself. You could always invent some good reason for leaving quickly, if that is what you intend to do."

"I had thought in fact, it would be wise to leave this afternoon. The yacht is moored near Westminster Bridge, and I can make an excuse for having to hurry away rather than dine with her this evening, as she expects me to do."

"I do see your predicament and if things are indeed as pressing as you say they are, then, dear boy, you must surely disappear and contrive to make your departure seem as plausible as possible."

"I felt certain that Your Royal Highness would help me," the Marquis muttered.

The Prince made a gesture with his hands.

"I have it!" he cried. "I know exactly how I can be of help to you! I will ask Lady Heywood to dinner tonight and when she arrives I will tell her that I have received a message from you saying that one of your close relatives is on the point of death. You have asked me to explain to her that you have had to leave London immediately."

"Brilliant idea and if you could do that, sir, it would be extremely kind of you and very helpful."

"Of course I can do it! I will send a message now asking Isobel to dinner. I feel sure that if she knows that you are having luncheon here with me, she will expect you to have been invited too."

"I am sure she will, sir, and Your Royal Highness thinks of everything and I cannot express to you in words how grateful I am."

"I am delighted to help you, Oliver, and of course I will make your apologies for not having sufficient time to be in touch with her. I will say that you only received the message of your relative's illness whilst you were here at luncheon."

"Thank you, sir, thank you very much."

The Prince rang a bell.

When a footman answered it, he instructed him to tell his secretary to send off a messenger at once to Lady Heywood's house inviting her to dinner tonight.

The footman hurried off and the butler announced that some other guests had arrived and they were with the Princess in the main reception room.

The Prince of Wales turned to the Marquis.

"I think we have settled that problem," he said with a tone of satisfaction.

"You have settled it for me, sir, and it has saved me a great deal of trouble. I have been wondering just what I could do about Isobel and I feel sure that you will offer her some consolation tonight when she dines with you."

"I will do my best, my dear boy, now come along. I have placed a specially attractive young lady beside you at luncheon today!"

As the Marquis walked behind the Prince towards the reception room, he thought he had been very astute.

He had now dealt in a skilful manner with Isobel.

He had undoubtedly prevented her from asking him the embarrassing question he feared and above all, he had made the Prince of Wales feel responsible for her, and that would soften the blow considerably.

'By the time I return to London,' he told himself, 'she will have found someone to take my place.'

It was an optimistic hope, but at the same time if he stayed away long enough he was certain that Isobel would not remain lonely.

He was not particularly interested in the new beauty that the Prince of Wales introduced to him, but there were a number of amusing and interesting people present.

The Marquis found himself forgetting the tension of last night and the even worse drama of this morning.

*

When he left Marlborough House he drove straight to where he knew his yacht would be waiting for him.

Mr. Foster and Bolton had done a very good job.

Everything he could possibly require on the voyage was already in its place on board *The Neptune*.

His valet, Gilbert, was waiting for him.

The Marquis was ceremonially piped aboard.

After he had been greeted by Captain Gordon, he was introduced to his wife.

She was getting on towards middle age, but she still had some of her youthful attractiveness and she had a soft, well educated voice.

She thanked the Marquis profusely for allowing her to accompany her husband on *The Neptune*.

"It has been one of my dreams, my Lord, to travel on a yacht captained by my husband and I can only thank you for the most perfect wedding present ever."

"I am so delighted to have you here, Mrs. Gordon. I expect your husband has arranged for the crew to drink your health this evening and then to enjoy the cake that I understand my secretary has managed to procure for you at short notice."

"It is the biggest wedding cake I have ever seen," Mrs. Gordon replied enthusiastically. "It is very gracious of your Lordship to think of it."

The Captain said the same and as the engines began to turn, *The Neptune* moved slowly out into the mid-stream of the river and down towards the sea.

Only then did the Marquis give a sigh of relief.

He had finally escaped and it had certainly been the most dangerous moment that he had ever had to face – yet he had settled it without a row or tears.

A little later he went out on deck.

All the tall towers and spires of the City of London were fast disappearing into the distance and small waves were beginning to splash against the bow of *The Neptune*.

The Marquis felt the exhilaration of being free and untroubled in a way he could not express in words.

'I am starting off on a new adventure,' he reflected. 'I will therefore not think of the past or what is happening in my absence. I will concentrate on what lies ahead and that, I feel, as it is all so new, will be an inexpressible joy.'

It was, he thought, when much later he retired to his cabin, a joy in itself to be alone.

Not only just because of the women like Isobel who invariably made relentless demands on him – also because he could not go for long without seeing his horses which were in training at Newmarket.

He always enjoyed being present on a Racecourse when any of them were likely to win.

He was a good polo player and polo had become a fashionable sport and there were always admirers watching him as he distinguished himself in the game.

Apart from his sport there were his many visits to Windsor Castle.

His father had occupied a most influential position at Court and it was only a question of time before Queen Victoria offered him a similar post.

The Marquis knew that she was only waiting until he was older and he had a slight suspicion that she was also waiting until he had married and 'settled down'.

He disliked that expression intensely.

He could see it would mean spending a great deal of time on his estate.

He would have to listen endlessly to his wife rather than to other women and he was sure that every tomorrow would be a boring repetition of yesterday.

Nothing new, unusual or exciting would be likely to happen to him.

If he went out to a dinner party or met a new face out hunting, that would be his only excitement.

He had very often thought to himself that the most stimulating thing about love affairs was the beginning.

The moment when he realised that someone looked a little different from the other females around her.

The first note of her voice and the sudden widening of her eyes when she realised how attractive he was.

He knew every single movement, yet each time it happened it seemed new, exciting and even thrilling.

Once he was tied up and married there would be no more of that – not only from his point of view, but from the women he met.

The unmarried man was certainly fair game and a woman knew exactly how to stalk him.

It would be very different when he was protected,

watched over and guarded by a wife and she could make things very unpleasant if she was jealous or suspicious.

When he was lying in bed, he listened to the sound of water lapping against the sides of the yacht.

He knew that by tomorrow he would be many miles away from London, from Isobel and any other woman he had left angry and frustrated because she had lost him.

'I am *free*,' he said to himself as he cuddled down against the pillows. 'And that is how I intend to remain.'

He then fell into a deep sleep almost before he had finished luxuriating in his glorious escape.

*

Captain Gordon had been told there was no reason to hurry.

So in the morning when the Marquis rose, it was a delight to find he could pay attention to the yacht itself.

He had always wanted his own yacht even when he was a small boy.

He had studied other people's yachts and one of the first enterprises he had embarked on when he had become a Marquis was to build *The Neptune*.

The first English yacht on record was *The Pearl* of ninety-five tons built in 1820 and another was *The Arrow* which was built two years later.

The Marquis was determined that his yacht, when it finally appeared, would be larger, swifter and more elegant than any of the others.

He had talked about it with the Prince of Wales as His Royal Highness had become President of the British Yacht Racing Association that had been founded in 1875.

Like the Marquis, he was extremely interested not only in the racing ability of a yacht, but that it should be as comfortable as a travelling house.

He insisted that if beautiful women were to sail in yachts, they must be as comfortable as in a Palace.

The sailing rules governing the handling of yachts while racing were strictly codified and had been approved by His Royal Highness.

The Marquis was flattered when the Prince asked his opinion as to whether he thought the rules were just and effective.

He decided that as soon as he returned to England after his journey to Scotland, he would invite the Prince of Wales to take a tour of inspection on board *The Neptune*.

He would also enter her in the next available race, provided she had every chance of winning.

'I must discuss this with the Captain,' he thought. 'It will be certainly something new for me to win a yacht race rather than a horserace!'

Then he laughed at the idea.

He had won so many trophies one way or another – so one extra prize for *The Neptune* would not make much difference.

Yet he could not help thinking at the very back of his mind that it was important he should keep himself well occupied by other interests rather than just women.

That Isobel had virtually proposed marriage to him had been a shock he would not forget in a hurry.

He now remembered a relevant incident –

A friend of his he had been at Oxford with had been out riding and a girl, who was a near neighbour and whom he had known for many years, joined him.

A violent thunderstorm had suddenly burst and they had sheltered in a small woodcutter's hut until the worst of the storm had passed.

Because they were both so interested in horses, they had talked about them during the hours they were together.

It had never even occurred to the Marquis's friend to kiss her.

Finally they returned home very late and the girl's family were most perturbed as to what had happened.

The following day her father called on the young man's father and had insisted that her reputation had been damaged. He stated firmly that the only way a gentleman could behave was to ask for her hand in marriage.

The Marquis's friend had been in despair.

"I quite like Elizabeth," he groaned. "She is a very pleasant girl and I have known her since I was a child, but I have no desire to marry her. What the hell can I do?"

"Have you explained what you feel to your father?" the Marquis had asked him.

"My father says," was the reply, "if I do not do the decent thing, it will besmirch the whole family and I will be branded as a cad for the rest of my life."

The Marquis had agreed to be his Best Man as there had been nothing else he could do for him.

He told himself then that if there was a storm when he was out riding, he would much rather be soaked to the skin than shelter from it with a woman!

*

Later that day a big storm blew up, but *The Neptune* proved more than able to cope with it.

The Marquis was never seasick, yet because there was a great deal of pitching and tossing, he learnt later that several of the crew had succumbed.

"I will pull into a harbour this evening, my Lord," suggested Captain Gordon. "There is just no point in being uncomfortable and it is in storms like this that one can run into rocks or collide with another ship."

The Marquis exclaimed in frustration.

"For Heaven's sake, Captain, must you! The yacht seems so perfect at present and that is how I want her to remain."

"So do I, my Lord, and you are not to worry. *The Neptune* is sounder and more dependable than any woman. She will not let us down."

The Marquis believed this to be true.

He enjoyed an excellent dinner in comfort while the yacht was anchored in a small harbour.

What was more the sea was subsiding and when he finished his meal he read a most interesting book on India.

Later he read several more chapters in bed before he turned out the lights.

He kept telling himself that he would not think of Isobel, but at the same time in the darkness, he could not help wondering what she was thinking and feeling.

He had no wish to make her unhappy, but he could not sacrifice himself merely to give a woman the pleasure of being his wife and sharing his title.

'When I am getting on for the ripe age of forty,' he reflected, 'I will begin to think seriously of getting married. That would give me ten more years of sheer enjoyment – untroubled, un-nagged and un-bored!'

The words seemed almost to roll off his tongue.

Then he chuckled.

He was being far too serious about what was really just a minor episode in his life.

There would undoubtedly be a great many more of his *affairs-de-coeur* yet to come.

'The only thing I have to avoid,' he mused before he fell asleep, 'is a trap. By now I should be quite sensible enough to recognise one on sight!'

*

The next day the sun was shining and *The Neptune* was moving swiftly and the Marquis spent most of the day on the bridge with Captain Gordon.

He heard stories about the sea and Scotland that he had never heard before.

When the Captain wished to go below, the Marquis took charge and he found controlling the yacht himself was as exhilarating as riding a spirited stallion.

By the time the day was over they had progressed a long way up the coast.

Tomorrow they would be in Scottish waters.

The Marquis debated whether he would stop off in Edinburgh as it was a City he really wanted to visit again.

He had read with much interest a new book which had described how much George IV had enjoyed a Royal visit to Edinburgh soon after he became King, when he had been welcomed with open arms.

'Perhaps I will go there on my way back South,' the Marquis pondered.

The Earl of Darendell would have by now received the letter he had told Mr. Foster to write and he would be expecting him shortly and it would be somewhat rude if he lingered too long on the journey.

He tried to remember what his father had told him about the Earl.

All he really knew was that Darendell Castle was of great historical interest and that the Earl himself came from an ancient family, the McDarens being one of the oldest and most respected Clans in the North of Scotland.

The Marquis had enjoyed fishing ever since he had been a small boy – he had fished in the lake at home and been thrilled when he caught even a small fish.

He could remember his first one and he had carried it excitedly back to his mother.

Later he had fished on the best rivers in England.

He had also fished abroad and there he had caught a variety of fish and had difficulty in discovering the names of some of them.

Now he recalled that his father had told him that the Daren River was one of the very best salmon rivers in the whole of Scotland.

The Marquis thought with satisfaction that at least he had brought the strongest rods and the finest collection of new flies that could be purchased in London.

It was far too early for grouse shooting and yet if he made himself pleasant he would doubtless be invited again for the twelfth of August.

'In point of fact,' he pondered, 'I am not going to miss London even for a second. It will be a change to be fighting for a silver salmon rather than for a pretty woman, who would doubtless not seem to be so attractive once I had caught her!'

Then he laughed at himself for being such a cynic.

At the same time he could not help rejoicing again and again that he was free.

And that was more important than anything else.

CHAPTER THREE

The next day was very rough again and when the yacht reached Holy Island, the Marquis decided he would definitely call in to Edinburgh.

They passed by the mouth of the River Tweed and although a strong head-wind was still blowing, the Marquis went on deck to watch *The Neptune* move slowly past St. Abb's Head.

From there they steamed along steadily up to North Berwick and then altered course to enter the Firth of Forth.

It was a little time before the skyline of Edinburgh came into view and the Marquis could see ahead of him the Palace of Holyroodhouse and Edinburgh Castle.

On the outskirts of the City they put into a harbour where there were a number of small boats sheltering from the bad weather.

The Marquis remembered distinctly that the house where he had stayed with his father was not far from the Palace.

As it was not yet late in the afternoon, he thought he would call on them immediately.

He sent a sailor on shore to find him a carriage and a few minutes later he was moving through the streets of Edinburgh.

He wondered if it might be interesting to call in at Edinburgh Castle, as there could be Officers there he had known in the past.

But then he decided it would be better to call first on his father's great friend, Lord McTranar.

The house was large and impressive exactly as he had remembered it.

He asked if Lord McTranar was at home and was shown into a room where there were a number of people.

When his name was announced, two men rose and the Marquis recognised them as old friends he had known as a boy.

"Oliver," one of them exclaimed, "this is indeed a big surprise!"

"I thought it would be, Neil, I am on my way to the North of Scotland in my yacht, but as the sea was so rough I put in here for shelter."

"And you remembered to come to us," Neil said in a tone of satisfaction.

He turned to the younger man next to him.

"I expect you remember my brother, Brian. He was not so large when you last saw him."

The Marquis held out his hand.

As he did so, it suddenly struck him that the Lord McTranar he remembered must now be dead and Neil must now be the Chieftain of the Clan.

This was confirmed when Neil added,

"I don't think you have met my stepmother."

A woman rose from the sofa who the Marquis saw at once was most attractive.

"I have heard the boys talk about you," she began, "but I never thought I would meet you."

"Well, fate or a rough sea has brought me now," the Marquis replied.

"And you must stay with us," insisted Neil. "We are

giving a dinner party tonight and it will be delightful for our friends to meet you."

"I am sure I shall enjoy meeting your friends. Are you sure you want me to stay? I can easily go back to my yacht."

"I insist you stay with us, Oliver."

He rang a bell and told the butler that the Marquis would be staying the night and a carriage was to be sent to the yacht to fetch his clothes and his valet.

"It is very exciting for us having you here," Lady McTranar said to the Marquis. "Whenever we have news from London, you always seem to be mentioned. The boys have told me so many stories of what fun you had when you stayed here when you were younger."

"I am glad I have not been forgotten – "

"I am sure it would be difficult for anyone to forget *you*," Lady McTranar replied.

There was a note in her voice that sounded familiar.

When he looked at her he recognised the expression in her eyes that he had seen so often.

It seemed most extraordinary that Neil's stepmother should be so young and the Marquis guessed she was about the same age as himself or perhaps just a few years older.

Yet she had been married to Lord McTranar whom he remembered as being the same age as his father.

The Marquis learnt that the party this evening was being given in honour of the Duke of Hamilton and several Scottish aristocrats from Edinburgh had also been invited.

After having no one to talk to for the last few days, the Marquis enjoyed the conversation which followed over a number of cups of tea.

Then Lady McTranar took him up the stairs and the Marquis realised immediately he was being put in one of the State bedrooms.

Waiting for him in the room was Gilbert with his evening clothes already laid out on a chair.

"I do hope you have everything you require," Lady McTranar said. "And your valet can ask for anything he requires from the servants."

"You are very kind," replied the Marquis. "And I am looking forward to a dinner I did not expect."

"Then let us hope you will not be disappointed."

She smiled at him beguilingly before she left him in the room to change.

Gilbert was delighted that he was staying on shore.

"You are very wise, my Lord, to turn in here. The Captain was saying before I left the yacht that it looked as though it'd be even rougher tonight than it were during the day."

"That is what I rather suspected and I am sure that we shall sleep very much better here than we would on *The Neptune*."

He realised when he had bathed and dressed that he was looking extremely smart as he walked downstairs.

The Duke of Hamilton had already arrived and he reminded the Marquis that the last time they had met was at Windsor Castle.

"I do not go South very often," he said, "and when I do, I usually get told off by Her Majesty for having done something wrong!"

The Marquis chuckled.

"I well remember my father wondering before he had an audience with Her Majesty what he had done and invariably it was something of which Her Majesty did not approve!"

They both laughed and then dinner was announced.

There were twenty people in all to sit down in the huge dining room with a minstrels' gallery at one end.

The Marquis found that he was on the left of Lady McTranar while the Duke of Hamilton was on her right.

Because she was looking extremely attractive, they both vied with each other in making her laugh.

She managed to flirt with them just as skilfully, the Marquis considered, as if she was one of the acknowledged beauties of the *Beau Monde*.

The Highland Games were scheduled to take place the following week and there was much conversation at the table about the athletic skills that would be on display.

The Marquis expressed his regrets that he could not stay and enjoy the Games.

"We would just love you to stay on if you possibly could," Lady McTranar murmured in an almost caressing tone.

"It is an event that I would really enjoy, but having accepted an invitation from the Earl of Darendell, I do not think it would be very polite to change my arrangements at the last moment."

"I can see you are very considerate and kind," Lady McTranar remarked.

"I try to be, and it would not be difficult to be kind to someone as beautiful as yourself."

"Now you are flattering me," she smiled, "but it is something I do enjoy. The Scots are rather slow at paying compliments."

"I cannot believe it where you are concerned."

Again she gave the Marquis that special look he was so familiar with.

Dinner finished with a speech from Neil McTranar, saying how much he appreciated being able to welcome the Marquis as his guest at the family home.

"He came here," he said, "when he was a boy, and since then he has become very influential and I understand has travelled a great deal. But we are delighted to think he has not forgotten Scotland and I want him to know that he is always welcome here whenever he finds time to cross the border."

To the Marquis's surprise there was applause at this remark from all the other guests.

When the ladies retired two distinguished Scotsmen told him that they fondly remembered his father and that they had always invited him to visit them whenever he had the time.

One of them owned an excellent grouse moor and the Marquis thought it very likely that by August he would be able to accept such an invitation himself.

They joined the ladies in the drawing room, which as usual in Scotland was on the first floor.

Lady McTranar came over at once to the Marquis.

"I thought we might play bridge and I would be so delighted if you would agree to partner me."

"Nothing would give me greater pleasure – "

They sat at the bridge table with another interesting gentleman and a very elegant lady.

To Lady McTranar's delight she and the Marquis won easily.

When their opponents said goodnight, they begged the Marquis to dine with them one day, so that they could have their revenge.

The rest of the guests did not stay long and it was not yet midnight when they all retired upstairs to bed.

"There is no need for us to be in any hurry in the morning," Neil told the Marquis, "but Brian and I wish to inspect your yacht from top to bottom. I hear it has all the modern gadgets and I would just love to see them before you leave."

"I will be delighted to show them to you. Perhaps you would like to come a little way with me on my voyage, but there is no hurry if it is still blowing hard."

He said goodnight to Lady McTranar and thanked her profusely for a delightful evening.

When he took her hand into his, he felt her fingers tighten on his and although it was such a familiar action, it surprised him a little.

Gilbert helped him undress.

Then because he had not slept a great deal the night before, the Marquis climbed into bed.

He was about to blow out the candles, when to his surprise the door opened.

For a moment he felt it must be Gilbert – maybe he could have left something behind and had come back for it.

Then as the newcomer did not speak, he turned his head.

To his astonishment he saw Lady McTranar.

She was looking extremely attractive with her soft auburn hair falling almost to her waist.

Slowly she walked towards him.

Then, as the Marquis stared at her, she murmured very softly,

"I came in to see if you were comfortable and had everything you wanted."

Just for a moment the Marquis was silent and then he replied,

"Not everything!"

*

The following morning the Marquis awoke early.

He could hardly believe that what had happened the previous night had been anything but a dream.

Having rapidly run away from Isobel, he had never imagined for a moment that anyone in Scotland would take her place so quickly.

It would have been impossible, he thought now, not to have been attracted by Lady McTranar.

She was not only incredibly beautiful, but lived up to the fiery colour of her hair.

It was an unexpected episode that any man would appreciate.

She had left two hours later in the same unexpected and quiet way she had arrived.

It was certainly something that the Marquis had not anticipated could happen at the very moment he set foot in Scotland!

He had, as he had only been there as a boy, thought of Scottish women as just kind and friendly.

But not particularly alluring or glamorous.

Lady McTranar had undoubtedly proved his views completely wrong!

He had to admit he had enjoyed every moment she had been with him.

Equally the Marquis told himself as he dressed that it would be a mistake to linger.

He was quite certain that the two brothers he had known as a boy would not expect their stepmother to be an attraction for him.

It was with a sense of relief that he realised the sun was shining and yesterday's storm had blown itself out.

When he went down to breakfast, he found only the gentlemen of the party were present.

"It's a nice and calm day," Neil greeted him, "and we are both longing to see your yacht."

"And that is what I will show you before I leave."

"You will come back for luncheon, Oliver?"

The Marquis shook his head.

"I think I must take advantage of the good weather to sail North. I would expect that I will have to shelter at night and that always means a delay."

Neil and his brother accepted this without arguing.

The Marquis had already told Gilbert to return to the yacht with his luggage.

When they were preparing to drive to the harbour, there was no sign of Lady McTranar.

"I think I should say goodbye to your stepmother," the Marquis suggested as he stepped into the carriage.

"She will not yet be awake," responded Neil. "But I have left a message with her maid to let her know where we have gone and I expect she will join us later."

The Marquis made no comment, as he was thinking that actually it would make it easier if he wrote to her later.

Gilbert had told the Captain they were coming and they were piped aboard and everything was shipshape and ready for their inspection.

Neil and his brother said that they were so delighted with everything they were shown.

The vast majority of all the modern innovations and changes the Marquis had installed on *The Neptune* had not yet reached Scotland.

Captain Gordon was clearly pleased at their praise of everything they saw as they went round the engine room and into every other part of the yacht.

At the end of the tour there were drinks waiting for them in the Saloon.

"I am determined now," said Neil, "that I will have a yacht, and I will try to make it even more magnificent and up-to-date than yours, Oliver."

"That is indeed a challenge, Neil, but I will be very annoyed if you succeed!"

They all laughed.

Then as *The Neptune* moved slowly out of harbour, they went up on deck and stayed on the yacht for another half-an-hour.

Then they said they must go ashore, as it might be difficult further on to find a conveyance to take them back.

The Marquis warmly thanked both Neil and Brian for a most enjoyable evening spent with them.

He then requested them to pay his respects to their stepmother and thank her for her kindness as she had not put in an appearance.

He thought it might seem strange if he suggested sending her some flowers.

He found a book in the Saloon which had recently been published about Queen Victoria and he thought it was something anyone would like to have in their possession.

He asked his Steward to pack it up and then he gave it to his friends to take back to Lady McTranar.

"She will be sorry she did not say goodbye to you, Oliver, but perhaps you will come and visit us again when you journey South."

"Yes, you must," Brian chimed in.

"You are both exceedingly kind and I will certainly accept your kind invitation if it is at all possible."

They said goodbye again being very complimentary about the yacht as they did so.

The Neptune moved slowly away towards the open

sea and the Marquis waved from the deck till they were no longer in sight.

It was a great relief when they left the Firth of Forth to find that the sea was comparatively calm and there was no sign of the storm rising again.

The Marquis spent the day with the Captain.

Then having dined alone, he went to bed in his very comfortable cabin, although it was not as impressive as the room he had occupied last night.

As he lay in the dark, the Marquis could not help thinking it was so extraordinary of Lady McTranar to come to his room on such a short acquaintance.

It was something he had never expected to happen in Scotland as he had always thought of the Scots as more elderly and very proper in their behaviour.

The situation had taken him so much by surprise that it was only now did he appreciate that Lady McTranar was a widow.

He had sworn never again to become involved with one!

However, it was, he thought, very unlikely she had any further interest in him except as 'a ship that passed in the night.'

He was young, he was attractive – and so was she.

He guessed if they had met each other unexpectedly in London the same thing would have happened.

It only seemed strange because it was in Scotland and in a house he had only known when he was a boy.

She was certainly most seductive and he supposed in a way it had helped him to forget how afraid he had been of Isobel and her demands on him.

Then he told himself that he had come to Scotland to forget women and to think only of sport.

'That,' the Marquis said to himself firmly, 'is what I will concentrate on in the future.'

He did not believe there would be many attractive red-headed Lady McTranars ahead of him.

If there were any, he must then be astute enough to avoid them.

*

The next day the sea was calm and the sun warm.

The Marquis enjoyed every moment of the clement weather.

The Captain had suggested that they might stop at Montrose, but the Marquis thought it would be wiser to sail on to Aberdeen.

Once there he knew that it would only take another day to reach Darendell and the Castle was situated in a bay only a short way from the River Daren.

He was looking forward to the salmon fishing as if he was once again a young boy.

He recalled learning from his father how to cast and looked back with pride at how proficient he had become and how many salmon he had managed to catch.

There had been small fish in the lake in front of his ancestral house in the country and in the clear stream that ran down the middle of the estate.

Although he had enjoyed proudly taking his catch back to his dear mother, it was not the same excitement as catching a salmon.

'I suppose I am really just a sportsman at heart,' the Marquis told himself.

He was thinking of the grouse he had shot over the years and the pheasants in his woods, as well as his horses which he enjoyed riding more than anything else.

Now he began to surmise that he had been spending far too much time lately in London chasing women, rather than enjoying himself in the fresh air of the country.

He felt that he was now almost accusing himself of being unsporting.

He reflected on the long hours he had spent with Isobel rather than with birds and beasts.

Then he laughed at himself for becoming pompous.

'It is part of my education, and by this time I must be nearly top of the form!'

*

It was three o'clock the next day when *The Neptune* moved slowly into the bay in front of Darendell Castle.

The Marquis had never seen a picture of the Castle, but it was so exactly how he felt a Highland Castle should look that it seemed almost familiar.

It was white against a green background of fir trees, raised above a garden massed with flowers.

The turrets on each side of the main block of the Castle made it most imposing and almost threatening.

In fact it came to the Marquis's mind it was a Fairy Castle and not real.

The Captain skilfully berthed *The Neptune* along a wooden jetty which stood out into the bay.

As soon as the yacht appeared, it was apparent that the Earl had members of his staff looking out for him and by the time *The Neptune* was safely moored, there was a man waiting to greet them at the end of the jetty.

A number of what the Marquis took to be footmen were also in sight and the young man waiting came aboard and explained he was the secretary to the Earl.

"His Lordship has been expecting you for the last two days, my Lord."

"We were delayed by a rather vicious storm," the Marquis explained "and turned into Edinburgh."

"That was a very sensible thing to do, my Lord, if I might say so. Those storms can be dangerous for a small vessel."

The Marquis stepped ashore.

He was taken through some beautiful gardens by the secretary and up a flight of steps that led to the Castle.

"His Lordship has been so looking forward to your visit, my Lord, and I am sure you will enjoy the fishing, which has been particularly good lately."

"I am much looking forward to the sport."

They entered the Castle by the front door and into a vast hall. It was hung with antlers and surprisingly there was the head of a tiger over the fireplace.

As if he was accustomed to making explanations, the secretary informed him,

"His Lordship killed several tigers in India and you will see their heads in various parts of the Castle."

The Marquis smiled.

He had thought of bringing back home the head of the tiger he had killed in India, but then he had decided it was too much trouble.

It might, however, have looked rather impressive in his house in the country.

They climbed up the wide staircase.

The secretary was still with him, but they had also been joined by a butler wearing a kilt.

Then throwing open a large door he announced in a stentorian voice,

"The Marquis of Kexley, my Lord."

The Earl was standing at the window looking over the garden at *The Neptune* in the bay.

He turned and the Marquis saw, with his white hair and lined face, that he had aged more than he had expected.

"It is delightful to see you, Oliver, after all these years and I only wish your father was with you."

"I wish so too," replied the Marquis. "But he often told me how spectacular your Castle is, my Lord, and I do realise now I see it there are not enough words to describe its beauty."

The Earl looked pleased.

"It is something I am very proud of, Oliver, and I only hope you will enjoy staying with us as much as your father enjoyed it the last time he came."

"He often spoke of it, telling me how he shot two outstanding stags and caught, I think, over twenty salmon."

"I believe it was more than that. Your father was a great fisherman and I do hope that you are as proficient as he was."

"It is just what I am hoping too, but it is something which can be easily proved one way or the other!"

The Earl laughed.

"That is very true, but we have been lucky lately in having more fish than I can remember for some years, and I am also told that the hatching of the grouse this year has been exceptional."

"You are indeed lucky, my Lord. Actually I have brought with me not only my own rods but my father's."

"Then you cannot fail to land a prize catch which, of course, will go down in the annals of Dardendell Castle for posterity!"

They both laughed and then the Earl suggested,

"Tea is awaiting us in the next room. My wife had an engagement this afternoon, but she will be back soon. My daughter, not surprisingly, is fishing."

They walked across the large room.

It had surprised the Marquis that the walls were all covered in books.

There was a portrait over the mantelpiece of one of the ancient Earls in full Highland regalia and another one of his wife wearing both a tiara and a plaid.

They entered the room next door that also had long windows overlooking the garden and the bay.

The Marquis noted that it was decorated completely differently. Here there were a number of pictures against the pretty Chinese wallpaper that had obviously been there for years.

The tea table was in front of the fireplace and the Marquis noticed at once that it was laid for four people.

This meant there was no one staying in the Castle except himself.

Although it was not exactly what he had anticipated he thought it might be to his advantage – as after what had happened in Edinburgh, he might have been in for another surprise.

He sincerely hoped not, as he wanted to concentrate on the sport – also to forget, here in the North of Scotland, all the problems and stress that had beset him in London.

However, because he was who he was, they turned up unexpectedly in other places as well.

"Now do sit down," the Earl was saying, "and tell me all about your horses. I often see you mentioned in the newspapers as running winners in the Classic races, and I remember it was a sport your father always enjoyed."

"I have indeed inherited some excellent racehorses

from my father. We do pride ourselves on having bred the finest horses to be seen anywhere."

"It does not surprise me, Oliver, your father always wanted the best and I suspect you do too."

"Of course I do," answered the Marquis. "It is only difficult to be certain that one is not being hoaxed."

He went on to tell the Earl, because he saw he was interested, about the races his horses had won recently and what he was hoping to achieve in the future.

They had been eating their tea for only a little while when the door opened.

A young girl came running in.

"I have caught six fresh salmon, Papa!" she cried. "And the largest one is ten pounds."

The Earl held out his hand.

"That is very splendid, Celina. Just what our guest wants to hear."

As if she had been unaware of his presence, the girl turned round.

The Marquis rose and held out his hand.

They both looked at each other in surprise.

The Marquis because he had no idea that the Earl had such a young daughter.

Or that she would be so beautiful!

She was, in fact, very different from any woman he had ever seen before.

There was a distinct touch of gold in her long hair.

Her face he could only admit as being lovelier than in any woman he could ever remember.

For a moment he could not place her looks and then he decided that her features were definitely those he would associate with Classical grace.

Her eyes, which seemed to almost sparkle with the brightness of the sun, were the soft grey of a morning mist.

As she ran into the room, Celina appeared to be no more than a child.

When the Marquis took her hand, he realised that she must be eighteen or nineteen.

"It has been a wonderful day," she enthused. "The fish were rising one after another. At first they would not take, but then after luncheon I seemed to hook one every time I cast!"

"It is just what we all dream about," remarked the Earl. "The Marquis is determined to beat every record. Is that not true, Oliver?"

"I will certainly do my best – "

He smiled at Celina as he spoke.

Then to his surprise she turned away.

He felt, although he must be wrong, that there was an expression of fear in her eyes.

'I must be imagining it,' he told himself.

Yet he was aware that when Celina sat down at the tea table, her head was bent over and she was no longer enthusing in an excited voice to her father.

As the Earl went on talking, the Marquis noticed that Celina never again looked in his direction.

He could not understand it and considered it very strange – there was no doubt that she was behaving quite differently.

She was no longer the excited child who had come back from the river having caught a large bag of salmon – she was now quiet, restrained and undoubtedly shy of him.

The Earl did not notice the change in his daughter's demeanour as he had so much to discuss with the Marquis.

He was reminiscing about his father and how their friendship had gone back to when they first went to Eton together.

"It was almost a revolutionary step in those days for me to be sent South to be educated," he was saying. "My dear father had the idea that if we were to beat the English which, as you well know, we have always tried to do, then we must know them better and defeat them if possible on their own ground!"

The Marquis chuckled.

"That was a difficult ambition for anyone!"

"It was extremely fortunate for me, for as soon as I arrived at Eton and I don't mind saying that I was rather nervous of the place, I made friends with your father. He prevented me from being teased too much over my Scottish accent and being what the English consider a barbarian!"

The Marquis chuckled again.

"They had forgotten all about those idiotic ideas by the time I went there, my Lord."

"You were lucky, Oliver, I received a great number of kicks and snubs for being Scottish. But when I became your father's close friend, everything was different."

"Because he was supporting you?"

"I believe actually it was because we were both so strong. The bigger boys might have easily defeated me if I was alone, but, as there were two of us, they gave up being aggressive after we had won several battles against them."

"I feel sure that must have pleased my father. He was always fighting for a worthy cause or helping someone weaker right up to the very end of his life."

The Earl nodded his approval.

"That is true, and I do hope you will follow in your father's footsteps."

The Marquis could not honestly say he had actually done so – he had merely allowed himself to be swept away by the women who fell into his arms like ripe peaches.

He would not have been human if he had not been amused and at times delighted by the attention they paid him and he wondered what his father would say now that he had run away.

Confronted with the same circumstances his father would have gone into battle, even if he was single-handed.

The Earl was still telling little anecdotes of what he and his kind friend had done together at Eton.

They had both gone on to Oxford University and there they had planned to travel together to many parts of the world when they had finished their education.

It was here the Earl sighed,

"But then your father came into his title earlier than expected and was obliged to remain at home to oversee his many possessions and taking his place at Court."

He paused for a moment before he added,

"You are very lucky, my boy, that Queen Victoria has not gobbled you up already, as she does most young gentlemen with an ancient title and a handsome face."

The Marquis smiled.

"I think the real reason, my Lord, why she pays me no attention is that she strongly disapproves of my flirting. Her Majesty is waiting for me to marry before offering me a position at Court. And that, I may say, suits me. I have no wish to be permanently on parade as my father was."

"I can well understand."

The Marquis suddenly became aware that, when he had mentioned the reason Queen Victoria had not offered him a position, Celina had glanced up for a moment.

Once again he could see fear in her lovely eyes.

'What can be frightening her?' he asked himself. 'I just cannot be as overpowering as all that. Could she have been told some unpleasant stories about my behaviour?'

It was a question he could not answer.

But it worried him as the Earl went on talking and Celina did not even glance in his direction.

It was then that he heard some sudden noises from outside the room.

A dog was barking and someone was shouting.

The Earl looked up.

"Moira must have now returned, and I am anxious for you to meet her, Oliver."

He could hear a woman's high-pitched voice giving someone instructions, although he could not catch what she was saying.

Then he noticed Celina stiffen and she put down the cake she was eating.

He could not be certain, but he had the oddest idea that her fingers were trembling.

'I must be imagining things,' he told himself.

Then the door opened.

The excited barking of a small dog grew louder as a woman entered the room.

"Oh, there you are, my dear," called the Earl. "I was beginning to wonder what had happened to you."

The woman came further forward.

It was then that the Marquis himself stiffened.

She was someone he had never expected to ever see again and yet here she was walking towards him.

It was eight years since he had last set eyes on her.

CHAPTER FOUR

The Marquis had been nineteen when he was asked by a friend he had recently met at Oxford if he would come and stay in the country for a cricket match.

He was spoken of as being an outstanding cricketer and had already been awarded his Blue.

Of course, in those far-off days he had yet not come into his father's title and was known as Viscount Kex.

He accepted the invitation because he loved cricket and enjoyed the attention he received from his admirers.

The friend who had invited him was the son of Sir Gerald Benson who owned a large estate in Hampshire.

The house was enormous and it was big enough to accommodate the whole cricket team as well as quite a few of their friends and relations.

The Marquis found he had a nice bedroom on the first floor with most of the other guests higher up and he guessed that this was due to the fact that he boasted a title.

Sir Gerald Benson was almost seventy years of age. He had been a widower for several years and was married a second time to a woman much younger than himself.

The house party danced the first night after dinner.

There was rather a shortage of girls and Sir Gerald promised that he would remedy this the following evening.

"We are having a really large party after the cricket match," he said, "for the simple reason I am quite sure that you will win it."

"We will be incredibly annoyed, Sir Gerald, if we don't," the Captain of the home team had replied.

He looked at the Marquis as he spoke and added,

"It will be up to you, Oliver."

"Now you are scaring me," the Marquis responded. "But I will do my best."

Owing to the shortage of female partners, he spent some time after dinner politely talking to his host.

"It is a great pleasure for me," said Sir Gerald, "to host a cricket match here. Although I know my son has not been chosen for your Oxford eleven, I am hoping you will help him, as it is a game I would like to think he can excel in."

"I will do what I can, sir," the Marquis had replied. "I think what Peter really needs more than anything else is practice."

After that they talked about horses and Sir Gerald asked if he would like to ride early in the morning before the match.

"You must not tire yourself," he counselled, "but I have some horses that I hope will please you. I know that your father owns a magnificent stable."

The Marquis had accepted the offer with delight.

Next morning he and Peter rose an hour earlier than the rest of the team and they rode in the paddock and over the flat fields beyond it.

The stallion the Marquis had been mounted on was an outstanding one with Arab blood, and he thought it was a horse he would always remember.

He enjoyed his ride so much that he was hoping his invitation to stay would be extended.

But when he reflected about it, it seemed rather an odd household.

Sir Gerald's son, Peter, was a great deal younger than his father, who then had married for the second time a woman who seemed too young for such an elderly man.

She was, he considered, rather good-looking and he imagined her to be getting on for thirty.

Peter Benson did not seem particularly interested in his stepmother, although he resented it when she spoke to him sharply about attending to his guests.

When they returned to the house after their ride, the Marquis and Peter went into the breakfast room.

Most of the guests had finished their breakfast.

"Where have you been?" they were asked.

Some of them were obviously a little annoyed that the Marquis had been taken out riding, as they would have enjoyed a ride too if they had been included.

Peter explained the reason by saying,

"My father is very determined that we will win the match today and he did not wish you to be tired out. If you want to ride, I am sure you will be able to do so tomorrow. After all as today is a Saturday we are expecting you all to stay until Monday morning."

Those who were feeling a bit disagreeable about the Marquis's ride cheered up, and the conversation naturally reverted to cricket.

When the Marquis viewed the cricket ground at the back of the house, he understood Sir Gerald's anxiety for the match to be a success.

It was apparently traditional that the Benson estate should stage a cricket match every year and the proceeds of the gate-money were handed to one of the most deserving charities in the County.

This year Sir Gerald was determined that the match should be more successful than usual and he had invited the majority of the players from Oxford University.

The County team had won a number of matches for the season and was therefore a formidable adversary.

There were special seats at the ground for the Lord Lieutenant and the other dignitaries of Hampshire and also plenty of room for members of the public.

It was a fine day and fortunately not too hot and at the same time quite a number of women had brought their sunshades with them.

The Marquis was very keen to distinguish himself and he was not surprised when he was put in to bat first.

When he had scored a hundred runs, everyone rose, clapped and cheered him and there was a loud groan from the crowd when he was caught out ten runs later.

However, his success was much appreciated by Sir Gerald and when it was time for luncheon, Lady Benson paid him so many gushing compliments that he felt quite embarrassed.

The Marquis had not asked her to dance with him on the previous evening and he reflected later that it would have been polite to have done so.

There had been a few attractive young girls in the party and when they retired to bed, Peter had teased him, complaining that he had had more than his fair share of them.

"They danced very well," he commented to Peter.

"And the one you spent so much time with was by far the prettiest and none of the rest of us had a chance!"

"She was an excellent dancer, but equally she had little to say for herself."

"You expect too much, Oliver!"

At the end of the day the Benson team had won but by only fifteen runs – it had been a close finish, even more dramatic than the Marquis expected it to be.

Sir Gerald was absolutely delighted and at dinner, which he hosted for both teams, he made a formal speech congratulating every player, most especially the Marquis.

He said he looked forward to seeing him playing at Lords and that he would be very disappointed if Oxford did not beat Cambridge by a large margin.

Those from Oxford clapped and cheered, and then the Captain of the other team replied to the speech.

He said they all hoped Sir Gerald would give them another chance next year to have their revenge.

Sir Gerald readily agreed to this suggestion, which meant more cheers.

The Marquis had been rather surprised to find that he was seated on the right of Lady Benson and he supposed that this signified that he must be the hero of the match.

"You must tell me about yourself," enquired Lady Benson flatteringly. "I just cannot think why Peter has not asked you here before."

"I will come here again if I get the chance, and I am determined, after seeing what a success it has been today, to ask my father to arrange a cricket match at home."

"I am sure it is something he will want to do, if you ask him nicely," Lady Benson fluttered her eyelashes.

"We always hold the Hunt Ball at our house," the Marquis remarked, thinking that it might interest her. "Our ballroom is quite enormous and we can accommodate more people than the Master can or anyone else in the County."

"And who do you like to be dancing with? Anyone in particular?"

"I like anyone who can dance well."

"Then as we are going to dance after dinner tonight, I hope you will ask me for a waltz, Oliver."

The Marquis thought it was really a rebuke because he had not done so last night.

Quickly he responded,

"I should be most honoured, and perhaps it would be correct for you to open the proceedings."

"That is a very good idea, as once we start dancing everyone will do the same."

As the ladies left the dining room, she turned to her husband,

"Now, Gerald, you are not to stay too long. We all want to dance and if you gentlemen start reminiscing about cricket, we will all go to sleep waiting for you!"

Sir Gerald chuckled.

"I know exactly what you are saying to me, Moira, and we will be with you in twenty minutes, I promise."

"I will accept your word," she replied. "And I will be very angry if you break it!"

She walked to the door and all the gentlemen rose to their feet.

As Lady Benson had predicted the older gentlemen immediately began to reminisce about the days when they were young boys and grossly exaggerated the scores they had made in various matches.

It was actually a good half-an-hour later before the gentlemen joined the ladies in the ballroom.

Lady Benson was there waiting for the Marquis and when he reached her side, she whispered,

"I have told everyone we are to open the dance and I have chosen a lovely tune I know you will enjoy as much as I do."

The Marquis put his arm round her waist and at the same time he was somewhat annoyed to see that Peter had quickly invited the pretty girl he had danced with last night to be his partner.

'I will ask her for the next dance,' he decided. 'She is undoubtedly better on the floor than anyone else.'

It was only seven dances later that he managed to partner her – she was obviously a great success tonight and enjoying every moment of it.

As soon as the dance was over, she had promised to dance with the Captain of the County team.

In fact whilst the Marquis was trying to manoeuvre another dance with her, he then found himself once again the partner of Lady Benson.

"You dance as well as you play cricket," she smiled at him appealingly. "And Peter tells me that you are also an outstanding rider."

"I am lucky enough to have some very fine horses to ride at home."

"I hope that you appreciate ours, and I thought that tomorrow we should all ride at about eleven o'clock in the morning. Then after luncheon is over, we might sail down the river which I am sure you will relish."

"It all sounds delightful," agreed the Marquis.

"That is what I wanted you to say. Just as I want you to feel that this is a very special party I hope you will enjoy more than any of the others you have attended."

"I assure that you it is already at the top of my list," the Marquis answered politely.

"I have a special horse I would like you to ride, it is one my husband gave me as a Christmas present last year. If we can arrange to have a race on our private Racecourse tomorrow morning, I am sure you will win on it."

"It sounds marvellous, Lady Benson, and I did not know you had a private Racecourse."

"It was my idea, and it was only finished about six months ago, but I am sure that it will be easy to arrange all sorts of races and the high jumps are excellent training for young horses."

The Marquis was intrigued.

They talked on about the Racecourse as the dance finished and he found, because they had so much to say to each other, he was now dancing for the third time with his hostess.

"I think you are very clever," Lady Benson said to the Marquis a little later in the evening. "And you excel at everything you undertake."

"I try to and, as you will appreciate, there is a great deal to learn now that I am at Oxford."

"I am sure that you will soon learn what is most important in life, Oliver."

He was about to ask her what it was, when someone came up to Lady Benson to say goodnight.

"I am afraid we have to leave."

"Oh, must you, General?"

"I am not as young as I was," he answered, "and as I have to read the lesson in Church tomorrow, I must have a good night's sleep or I will stumble over the words."

"I am sure you would never do that!" Lady Benson assured him.

When she was occupied by talking to the General, the Marquis had another quick look round for the girl who danced so well.

He was irritated to observe that once again she was dancing with Peter and he was just about to select another partner when Lady Benson put her hand on his arm.

"I am longing for a glass of champagne, Oliver, and

I am sure you would enjoy one too. Let us go to the buffet in the room next door."

There was nothing the Marquis could do but agree, and he had to admit that the champagne was excellent.

Lady Benson insisted on him having a second glass.

They did not go back into the ballroom until they heard the band playing '*God Save the Queen*'.

"My husband thought it was a mistake for us to go on dancing when it was Sunday," Lady Benson explained when the Marquis looked somewhat surprised. "I told him he was being rather old-fashioned, but he did not want to offend the Bishop who was dining here tonight."

The Marquis had not noticed the Bishop earlier, but he could well understand Sir Gerald's reasoning.

The local guests started to say goodnight, but they all took a long time to depart and it was almost one o'clock before the house party retired to bed.

The Marquis looked for his hostess and found her closing the doors of the conservatory.

"Please help me," she asked. "The flowers are very precious and the cold night air is not good for them."

The Marquis helped her close the doors and when they had finished, he realised that most of the rest of the party had gone upstairs.

"Goodnight," he said to Lady Benson, "and thank you very much for a delightful evening."

"You were the real hero of the hour and the greatest success," she replied to him softly. "But although you are an expert in so many things, there is one that I do think you are rather ignorant about."

The Marquis felt surprised.

"What is it?" he enquired.

She looked up at him and placed her hand onto his shoulder.

"It is *love*," she whispered.

The way she spoke and the way she looked made him draw in his breath.

Then before he could respond, he heard Sir Gerald call out,

"Moira, where are you?"

Lady Benson turned towards him, then looked back at the Marquis.

"I will finish what I was saying," she murmured, "a little later on and that will complete what has been a very wonderful day."

Before the Marquis could say anything, she slipped away from him and ran back towards her husband.

The Marquis stood still gazing after Lady Benson feeling bewildered.

Could she possibly have meant what she said?

He could not believe it and yet the expression in her eyes had been very revealing.

At this stage in his life the Marquis had in fact had nothing to do with any woman.

There were a number of girls living near his home, who had come to the parties when he was a child and they turned up on special occasions, such as Christmas and Guy Fawkes Day.

But he had never thought that there was anything particular about them, nor was he, at this moment, friends with any girl unless she was a good rider.

Some of his contemporaries at Oxford had talked to him about their success with women, but he had not been interested as there was so much more to occupy his mind.

When he was at home, he always spent more of his time riding than anything else.

Now, as he went up to bed, he told himself he must have imagined what Lady Benson had said to him.

Equally he could not explain away the conviction that she intended to come to his bedroom.

Peter was just ahead, walking to his room at the end of the passage.

"Goodnight, Oliver," he called. "You were such a smashing success today, but I am too tired to talk about it now."

"Goodnight," the Marquis replied and went into his bedroom.

The candles were lit by the side of the bed and his nightshirt was left out for him.

Then as he was standing irresolute in the doorway, he suddenly panicked.

If Lady Benson was really coming to his bedroom – what was he expected to do?

What was she asking of him?

He was certainly not so ignorant he did not know the answer to that question – it was just impossible for him to believe it.

'If I shut the door and lock it,' he thought, 'then no one can disturb me.'

He had naturally closed the door as he entered the room and now as he turned back, he realised that there was no key – it seemed incredible that the lock was there, but the key was missing.

It was just then that he realised he somehow had to save himself from what could be exceedingly embarrassing if nothing else.

Swiftly he picked up his nightshirt and blew out the candles and then ran down the dimly lit corridor.

Without knocking he walked into Peter's room. He had been there earlier in the day when they were dressing for the match and had noticed there were two beds.

As he entered, Peter who was half undressed looked up in surprise.

"Oh, it's you, Oliver. What's the matter?"

"I have just upset a jug of water over my bed, and it has made it very wet and I don't want to catch a cold. Can I sleep in here with you?"

"You must be incredibly clumsy or drunk," laughed Peter. "But, of course, you may sleep here as long as you don't snore!"

"I promise you I never snore, and as you say, after all that champagne, my hand must be a bit unsteady."

"Get into bed and sleep it off, Oliver!"

The Marquis did as he was told.

But he found it impossible to go straight to sleep.

He kept wondering to himself if he had imagined the whole situation and yet he was sure that was what Lady Benson intended.

'I must get away from here at once,' he thought.

It would be impossible, if she had gone to his room, for him to face her again.

At six o'clock the next morning, he slipped out of bed and collected the clothes he had worn for dinner from a chair where he had thrown them.

Peter was fast asleep and snoring lightly.

There was just enough sunlight coming between the curtains for the Marquis carrying his clothes to see the way to the door.

Very softly he shut it behind him and walked back to his own room, which was just as he had left it.

There was nothing to show if anyone had come into the room whilst he was absent, except for just one thing – the key had been put back in the lock of the door!

It took the Marquis only a short time to dress and he packed his belongings into his suitcase.

He had arrived at Sir Gerald Benson's house in an open chaise driving two horses, and his father had insisted he took one of the older grooms with him so that the horses would be properly looked after.

"I am certain that they will be well cared for at the Bensons' house," the Marquis had protested.

"I am not trusting my superb horses to any strange grooms," his father had replied. "So take Abbey with you, and if you are too drunk to drive yourself, you know you can trust him to bring you home safely!"

"I am not going to make a fool of myself, Papa, by drinking too much. You know that is a grave mistake for any athlete to make."

His father had put his hand on his shoulder.

"Of course, I would trust you not to make a fool of yourself. Equally I do know what these parties can be like and the champagne good or bad will flow, especially if the Benson team win the match!"

His father had indeed been right.

The Marquis had noticed one or two of the players stumble when they left the dining room and he felt that he had been wise enough to keep his wits about him.

When he reached the stables a young, rather sleepy-looking groom looked at him in surprise.

"You be early, sir."

"I wonder if you would be very kind and find my groom."

The Marquis explained where Abbey would be and the young groom ran off to find him.

By the time Abbey arrived, the Marquis had taken the two horses out into the yard and had bridled them.

Abbey was sensible enough to ask no questions and he quickly produced the chaise and then minutes later they were ready to leave.

It was only at the last moment that the Marquis had remembered he must make some explanation to his host.

By this time a senior groom had appeared and the Marquis told him he had received an urgent message from his home saying he was wanted immediately and therefore he had to leave at once.

"Please will you inform Sir Gerald that I will write to him tonight with an apology."

"I'll tell 'im for sure, my Lord, and I 'opes you 'ave a safe journey."

"Thank you very much," the Marquis answered as he climbed into the chaise.

As he drove away down the drive, he felt somewhat ashamed of himself for being so cowardly as to run away, but then he was sure that he had done the right thing.

Lady Benson was the stepmother of one of his close friends.

However *she* might behave, *he* would certainly do what he thought was right and proper.

As he drove home he knew there was one thing he would regret more than anything else and that was losing his friendship with Peter.

It would be a mistake for him to visit Peter's house again and a mistake for him to come to his.

His father would doubtless think it polite to invite Peter's father and stepmother to stay, especially if the two boys were taking part in a cricket match, a steeplechase or hosting a party for the Hunt Ball.

The Marquis sighed.

He was fond of Peter, but he could not tell him the truth. He would have to let their friendship just drift away slowly, so that it did not seem in any way suspicious.

As he drove on he knew that he wanted to be back safely at home, and he told himself firmly it was vital that whatever happened in the future he must *never* meet Lady Benson again.

*

All of this had happened over eight years ago and the Marquis had almost forgotten the whole scenario.

Now, as his hostess came into the room he felt as if a bomb had exploded at his feet.

She walked over to her husband and bending down kissed his cheek.

"I am sorry to be late, but it was impossible for me to get away earlier. You know how women talk."

"I do indeed, my dear, but our guest has arrived in a magnificent yacht and I know you will want to meet him."

The Countess of Darendell held out her hand.

"I believe we have met before," she muttered.

She was looking straight into the Marquis's eyes.

As he looked back at her, he knew without being told that she hated him.

He could see it in her eyes and feel it in the touch of her hand and he had always been aware of other people's vibrations, especially those with strong personalities.

He recognised now that she had never forgiven him for humiliating her and refusing her advances.

'Then *why*, why,' he mused, 'has she permitted her husband to invite me here to the Castle?'

He could find no answer to this question.

The Countess related amusingly what had happened in the Village Hall.

The Earl was listening and it was impossible for the Marquis not to as well, but he was conscious that Celina had not looked up from her plate although she had stopped eating.

When there was a short pause in the conversation, she pushed back her chair and rose to her feet.

"I am going out into the garden, Papa," she said and turned towards the door.

Her father did not answer.

The Marquis was once again aware that there was an expression of fear in Celina's eyes, and he had not been mistaken in thinking her hand was trembling.

'*What* is upsetting her? What is wrong?' he asked himself.

Then his thoughts were back with his own problem as to what he should say to the Countess.

When tea was over, they moved back into the room where the Marquis had first met the Earl.

"There is an excellent view from here of our guest's yacht," the Earl was saying. "And I am hoping we shall be able to inspect it tomorrow."

"Of course you must, and I expect that you will be interested in some of the improvements I have made that as far as I know are not being installed into any other yacht afloat at the moment."

The Earl chuckled.

"You are just like your father, Oliver, I remember he always wanted to be a pioneer and eventually the first man on the moon."

The Marquis laughed at the Earl's comment, but it was rather a forced sound, and he was aware the Countess was looking at him.

He had by now regained his composure and had, he reckoned, recovered from the shock of seeing her again.

"I have always heard from my father how beautiful your Castle is," he said to the Countess, "and it was so very kind of you to have invited me to Scotland."

"I thought that you would be surprised to see me," she replied. "I expect you remember that cricket match in which you were undoubtedly the hero of the day."

"Of course, I remember it, but Oxford is such a big place that later I did not see much of Peter."

The Countess gave him a somewhat sarcastic smile, as if she realised the true reason.

Looking at her quizzically, the Marquis realised she had certainly grown older with the passing years. Now she undoubtedly looked nearly forty which he was certain was about her real age.

However, she was fashionably dressed with pearls around her neck and in her ears and her face was skilfully made up.

It was quite obvious that her husband, the Earl, was very pleased with her.

He was regarding her admiringly.

"I suppose, dearest," he said, "that you have asked some guests here to amuse our friend Oliver. From what the newspapers tell me he is of great standing in what in my day was called the 'Beau Monde'."

"I would expect it still is," the Marquis answered. "I was asked for luncheon with His Royal Highness the day before I left, and I can assure you he keeps the Social ball rolling so fast that one is constantly running from one party to another."

"I am sure he does so and who is he is love with at the moment?"

"I think his affair with the Countess of Warwick is still happening, but one can never be sure with His Royal Highness. His heart is a very large one!"

The Earl laughed and then the Countess enquired of the Marquis in a slightly affected voice,

"And what about *your* heart?"

The Marquis knew it was a pointed question and he replied,

"It is intact, thank you, and that is the way I wish to keep it."

The Countess raised her eyebrows.

"Can that really be true? Surely there is one beauty more alluring than any of the others you find irresistible."

The Marquis wondered what gossip she had heard about him.

Of course, so many people would tittle-tattle about Isobel and him just as they would have talked if they could about every other beauty he had had an affair with.

"You must not listen to the gossip," he said firmly. "I assure you that there is no one of any great importance in my life and I intend to 'play the field' for a great number of years yet."

The Countess sniggered and it was an unpleasant sound.

"Do you really expect me to believe that?"

"Whether you believe it or not, it is the truth."

"But I am sure that your family," she then persisted, "are really longing for you to marry and produce an heir. How can you do anything else when you have so much to be responsible for?"

"My family, like all other families, always concern themselves with matters that are not their business."

She laughed and again it was a discordant sound.

"To put it very simply, you are not married and you intend not to be – "

The Marquis so wanted to tell her to mind her own business, but knew it would be rude.

Instead he parried,

"I would presume that is obvious."

"I find it hard to believe. Even here in the North of Scotland we have heard and read about your success with the most beautiful women in London. Someone was telling me the other day about one of your conquests. Now what was her name? I am almost sure she was called Isobel!"

The Marquis so wished that he could tell her to shut up, but he merely smiled.

"If you want a list of the most beautiful women in London, I will gladly supply it. Without any photographs, which unfortunately I have not brought with me, it would be difficult for you to realise how gorgeous some of them really are."

The way he spoke and the look in his eyes told the Countess he had drawn swords with her.

He had, in fact, declared war.

She gave a little laugh and rose to her feet.

"You must tell me more another time. Now I must obey my husband and find some Scottish beauties. It will not be easy, but I would hate you to be disappointed – "

She walked from the room as she finished speaking.

As the door closed behind her, the Earl remarked,

"I had no idea you had met my wife before, Oliver, but I was, of course, very fond of your father and when she suggested I should invite you to stay here, it made me feel it was something I should have done long ago."

"I am so grateful, my Lord, for the invitation and I am looking forward to your salmon fishing."

"Let's hope that they do not elude you and Celina will be able to show you the best pools on the river. She is more experienced than any of the ghillies."

When the Marquis went upstairs to dress for dinner, he was thinking hard.

If he had known he would meet Lady Benson under another name, he would not have come and he was quite certain she despised him for the way he had spurned her all those years ago.

It seemed strange therefore that she had encouraged her husband to invite him to Darendell for the fishing.

It was unfortunate that she should be here to spoil the peace and quiet that he was looking for after his escape from Isobel.

From what she had just said, he suspected that one of her London friends had talked about him, and she knew far more than he wanted her to know.

There was, however, nothing he could do about it now and it was of little use to worry much over something that had happened so long ago.

After all he had been very young and inexperienced at the time and it would have been far easier to accept her advances than to refuse them.

Yet at that age and because she was married to an elderly man, he had thought of her as a much older woman.

That was until the moment in the conservatory.

Looking back now he remembered vaguely hearing that Sir Gerald Benson had died after an accident on his

Racecourse – apparently his horse had fallen at a fence and rolled on its rider.

By the time this had happened he had ceased to see anything of Peter and therefore he had not been particularly concerned.

Sir Gerald's death, however, had left his wife free to marry someone else.

The Marquis could well understand, as she was still fairly attractive, the Earl of Darendell being captivated by her, while she had undoubtedly desired his title.

The Marquis was thinking out the whole sequence of events, almost as if he was putting a puzzle together and he wondered if she really hated him for having refused her advances so long ago.

It was, as far as he was concerned, an event he had almost forgotten and he supposed that now he would laugh at the idea of avoiding her.

He would just have accepted whatever fate or the Gods brought him.

'I was young, innocent and somewhat foolish.'

Equally he was still rather shocked that a so-called respectable lady should offer herself to any man.

In his *affaires-de-coeur* the Marquis liked to think that *he* made the advances and that he enticed the beauty concerned into his arms, not that *she* enticed him.

It was not entirely the truth, in fact very far from it, but it was what he wanted to believe.

"This be a fine Castle, my Lord," Gilbert broke in on the Marquis's thoughts.

"I am impressed by it," he answered, "and I hope the staff here are looking after you properly."

"They seem friendly enough, my Lord, and that be usual where the Scots are concerned."

"Have you been to Scotland before, Gilbert?"

"My first position before I came to your Lordship's father were in Scotland. The gentleman that employed me lived near to Edinburgh and I was sorry when he went on a tour round the world and I then had to find myself another position."

"Is that why you came to my father?"

Gilbert nodded.

"He gives me a really excellent reference, and when your father took me on, it were exactly what I was wanting, especially when I could look after your Lordship."

The Marquis thought he would find it very difficult to do without Gilbert and, as he trusted him, he suggested,

"Find out a little more about the family, Gilbert. I know I can trust you to do it tactfully. I do not understand why Lady Celina, who can only be seventeen or eighteen, looks so frightened. And why the Earl, at his age, married such a young wife for the second time."

"It certainly seems a bit of a puzzle, my Lord, but leave it to me. There's nothing I enjoys more than finding out the reason for things what seems strange."

The Marquis gave a little laugh.

"There is plenty of it about, Gilbert, where we are concerned."

"Yes, I knows that, and there's no reason for us to feel down about anything at all. As I've said often enough, whatever might happen, your Lordship always comes out on top!"

"I only hope you are right, Gilbert."

CHAPTER FIVE

The Marquis caught four salmon on his first day on the river and Celina, who was with him, caught three.

He hoped, when they were going to the river that he would have a chance of talking to her.

He wanted to ask her what made her so frightened, but they each had a ghillie beside them all the time.

At luncheon time the Earl came down to the river to join them and they ate in a small wooden hut that had been built beside one of the best pools.

He insisted on watching them fish for a while after luncheon and then drove back to the Castle with them.

The Marquis noticed that Celina was completely at ease with her father. She laughed and talked with him and was apparently enjoying every moment.

She seldom looked at the Marquis directly and he was quite certain that when she did so, the fear was back in her eyes.

'Whatever can I have done,' he asked himself, 'to be such a *menace*?'

There was no obvious answer to that question.

Later Gilbert was a little more enlightening.

He informed the Marquis that the Castle household disliked their new Mistress and they thought that she was unnecessarily unkind to her stepdaughter.

"What do you mean, 'unkind'?" the Marquis asked as he was brushing his hair.

"They just wouldn't go into any details in front of me, my Lord, but I thinks there's something strange going on, although I can't guess yet what it is."

"Well keep on trying – and why do the staff really not like the Countess?"

"From what they said and they didn't confide in me much seeing as I'm a foreigner coming here from England. They thinks that she caught the old man, so to speak, and, as your Lordship's rightly said, there's a big difference in their ages."

The Marquis suspected that Moira Benson had been anxious to obtain a more significant title than Sir Gerald had given her.

There were guests for dinner the first night and the Marquis again did not get a chance to talk to Celina.

*

He had learnt, and it was a relief, that the Countess did not like fishing, so therefore the next morning he and Celina set off alone again.

They were in an open conveyance and there was no possibility of having a private conversation with her as the two ghillies could hear everything they said.

The Marquis was not so successful with his rod that morning, catching only one salmon and losing two, whilst Celina once again landed three salmon.

The Earl teased him over luncheon.

"You will just have to pull up your socks, Oliver, or otherwise Celina will have better marks than you and I am certain that you do not like being beaten by a woman!"

"It all depends on who she is – "

The Marquis tried to smile at Celina as he spoke.

But Celina had turned her head away and was not looking at him.

'What can be worrying her?' he asked himself.

It could scarcely be his appearance, as he had often been told ever since he was a boy that he was handsome.

The women he had made love to had always been extremely complimentary. He had been compared dozens of times to a Greek God.

There was not a single woman of his acquaintance who had not made it very obvious that she was proud to be with him.

Whether it was on the dance floor or in the park, he was smarter and better looking than any of the other men in sight.

*

The next night the guests for dinner consisted of the Earl's neighbours.

One gentleman guest was clearly a talker and had a great deal to say.

Dinner was coming to an end when the man sitting on the left of the Countess asked,

"Whatever has happened to Hambleton? I have not seen him for some time and I thought he used to be a friend of yours."

"I have not seen him either," replied the Countess.

As she was speaking the Marquis, who happened to be looking at Celina, saw her start visibly.

He could almost swear that her face had suddenly gone very pale.

"I never did care for him myself," the man on the other side of the Countess was saying. "I always suspected him of being cruel to his horses. At the same time he spent a great deal of money in the neighbourhood, and we miss him for that if nothing else."

"I would expect he will turn up sooner or later," the Countess remarked in a comforting voice.

"Like a bad penny," the man opposite remarked and then added, "or rather a golden sovereign!"

The Countess gave a little laugh and then changed the subject.

Watching Celina, the Marquis noticed that she took some time to relax and return to her normal self.

He always enjoyed a puzzle and a riddle, and found himself thinking that Mr. Hambleton, whoever he may be, must have upset her in some mysterious way.

But that was no reason why she should be so afraid of him.

'I must get an opportunity to talk to her,' he mused.

He then determined that he would most likely have a chance the following day which was Sunday.

This meant they could not go out fishing.

*

The Earl informed him at breakfast time that they were invited to luncheon at another Castle about ten miles away.

The Marquis felt interested in seeing this Castle and he wondered if it would be as attractive as Darendell.

They drove there in an open carriage with the Earl and Countess sitting on the seat facing the horses.

The Marquis and Celina were opposite them and he would have been very stupid if he had not realised that she sat as far away from him as possible.

She almost squeezed herself against the other side of the carriage and thus there was no chance of speaking to her before they arrived for luncheon.

The Castle was not that impressive, but it was very old, and situated on a lake, it had a charm all of its own.

There was a fairly large party for luncheon and they talked incessantly of sport and they were interested to hear how the Marquis was faring on the River Daren. There was also a lengthy discussion about which flies were the most successful in attracting the salmon.

They spoke about the grouse hatching and whether the bags would be as good as they had been last year.

It was interesting enough chat, but at the same time, as they drove home, the Marquis found himself once again worrying about Celina.

She had very certainly been the life and soul of the younger members of the family at luncheon. They had sat at the other end of the table while he was on the right of his hostess.

He could hear Celina's laughter and her soft, clear voice making those around her animated.

'What could I possibly have done,' he questioned, 'to make her behave so strangely with me?'

It was exactly the same on the return to Darendell Castle – again she sat as far away from him as she could.

Whenever he spoke directly to her, she answered in monosyllables without looking at him.

When they arrived, she disappeared quickly leaving him to follow slowly with his host and hostess.

That evening, when he was dressing for dinner, the Marquis again asked Gilbert if he had found out anything more about the family.

He would never have had such a conversation with any other servant, but Gilbert had been with him so long – in fact he always thought he was almost part of the family.

"Well, from what I gathers, my Lord, Lady Celina were as nice as possible when the Earl first married Lady Benson, but things have changed in the last month or two."

"In what way?" enquired the Marquis.

"Them be still not what your Lordship might call open-mouthed with me, but they hinted there be something unpleasant happening to Lady Celina that comes from her stepmother."

"Unpleasant? What could they mean by that?"

"One of the housemaids who's been here years, did say that her mother'd turn in her grave at what's going on. Then as if she'd already said too much, the other servants hushed her into silence."

The Marquis was intrigued – it was very definitely a puzzle he must solve, because in a way it concerned him.

"Just go on finding out what you can, Gilbert, and I hope you are comfortable here."

"Very comfortable, my Lord, now I've changed me room."

"Changed your room?"

"Well, it were just like this, my Lord. They puts me upstairs with the other menservants in what us calls in England, the attic. So I pointed out that if you wanted me, there was no way you could get in touch with me and it'd take me a month of Sundays to get to your Lordship."

The Marquis laughed.

"Then I insisted they move me," Gilbert carried on, "and now I'm in a small dressing room, which they say is very seldom used – just across the passage."

"That is certainly convenient, Gilbert."

"It suits me, my Lord, and if your Lordship shouts loud enough, I can hear you."

The Marquis laughed again as it was so like Gilbert to get his own way in whatever he wanted.

He appreciated it that the man liked to be near him

and Gilbert certainly looked after him better than any other servant could possible have done.

He went down for dinner and found the two guests who had come from nearby were a charming couple – he had met them before in England and they were delighted to see him again.

They talked animatedly about the parties they had attended in Mayfair and the people they both knew.

Then the lady, a Mrs. McCleod, asked,

"I think, that at the party where we met, you were with Lady Heywood. How is she? I think she is one of the most beautiful women I have ever seen."

"She is a great success," replied the Marquis. "The day I left London she was dining that night at Marlborough House."

Mr. McCleod chortled.

"Then I'm sure the Prince of Wales, who has an eye for a pretty woman, appreciates her."

"I would not be surprised, but he is still very much enamoured, I understand, with Lady Warwick."

The conversation then turned to the Prince of Wales and the Marquis was rather amazed at how well informed the McCleods were, despite the fact that they were so far from London and only crossed the border occasionally.

When dinner was finished the ladies moved into the drawing room, while the gentlemen stayed for some time talking about sport.

The Marquis learnt that Mr. McCleod boasted some fine stalking on his land, but fishing in his lake was not as interesting or as prolific as fishing in the river.

"When the Marquis leaves me," the Earl said to Mr. McCleod, "you must come and have a day on the Daren. I never have more than two rods fishing at the same time."

The Marquis smiled.

"Are you suggesting, sir," he asked the Earl, "that I have overstayed my welcome?"

"No, of course not. I would like you to stay for at least another two weeks and if you have not had a record catch by that time, I shall be disappointed."

"So will I and I am most grateful to you."

When they then rejoined the ladies, it was to find that Celina was not there.

The McCleods did not stay long.

"I always prefer to take my time driving back in the dark," said Mr. McCleod. "It is easy to have an accident if there is no moon and the horses are going too fast."

"You are most wise," agreed the Earl. "I am only sorry you must leave us."

"It's getting on for half-past eleven," Mrs. McCleod chipped in, "and I have reached the age when I enjoy my beauty sleep."

"So do I," agreed the Countess. "But please come and visit us again soon."

"We will come whenever you ask us," replied Mr. McCleod, "and I do hope your husband will not forget his invitation for me to fish on the Daren."

Both the McCleods then wished the Marquis 'good sport' and 'tight lines' and departed in their chaise.

What a pleasant and delightful couple they were for the Earl to have as his neighbours, he reflected.

"Now I suppose we must go to bed," he said.

"There is no hurry," asserted the Countess. "I am sure Ewen wants a nightcap and you will enjoy one too. I have made my 'special' for both of you."

She then said goodnight to the Marquis and left him and the Earl alone.

They walked to the grog table and the Earl picked up a glass, waiting for the Marquis to do the same.

The Marquis, however, hesitated as he felt he had drunk enough at dinner and actually disliked drinking just before he retired to bed.

The Earl sat down in a chair.

Deftly the Marquis pushed the drink left for him to one side and picked up an empty glass.

There was a large jug of lemonade on the tray and he filled the glass.

As he did so, the Earl spoke to him,

"I have been wondering, Oliver, just why you never married. I heard tonight the name of yet another beautiful lady you have been with, and they never seem, from what I have heard, to last long where you are concerned."

"I have no intention of getting married. The more my relatives beseech me to do so, the more stubborn I find it makes me. I do prefer being a bachelor and I will not be bullied up the aisle!"

The Earl put back his head and guffawed.

"You sound very much like your father who always had his own way in everything. Of course, you are quite right, my boy. Enjoy yourself while you are young – one is old for a long time."

"I am only too ready to take your advice, my Lord."

He next deftly turned the conversation back to the sport.

It was half-an-hour later before they went upstairs.

The Marquis was aware as they climbed slowly up the stairs that the Earl was somewhat unsteady.

He wondered what had been in the 'night-cap' and was glad he had not touched it.

The lights had already been dimmed to only three sconces in his passage, his own room being in the opposite direction to that of the Earl.

They said goodnight at the top of the stairs and as the Earl was tottering, the Marquis watched him until he reached his bedroom.

Then he walked towards his own room and opened the door.

He turned round to close it and then as he moved a little further into the room he came suddenly to a standstill.

He stared in front of him in sheer astonishment.

His large four-poster bed had a large ornate canopy over it.

Beneath it sitting up against the pillows was Celina!

For a moment the Marquis could not move and was speechless.

Then Celina spoke in a little voice that was hardly audible,

"I am sorry – I am – terribly sorry."

"What on earth are you doing *here*, Celina?"

"I am so sorry," she whimpered again, "and please, please – please don't be angry. It is not – my fault. I knew you would be horrified, my Lord."

"I am not horrified, Celina, just astonished."

"I thought you would be, but – *she* made me and I had to do – what she said."

The Marquis now reached the bed and sat down at the end of it.

He realised, as he did so, that Celina, who was only wearing a thin transparent nightgown, shuddered.

She seemed in the light of the candles to have gone even paler than she was already.

Deliberately keeping his voice as low and calm as possible, the Marquis enquired,

"Now, tell me from the beginning why you are here and why you have been frightened of me ever since I came to stay at the Castle."

"I was frightened," she answered, "because I knew just what she was going to do – and why she had asked you to come."

"I suppose you are referring to your stepmother?"

"Yes – and I so wanted to warn you, my Lord – but I could not do it once you had arrived."

"Now tell me what your stepmother wants and why you are here," the Marquis asked her very quietly.

"It is because tomorrow she will force Papa – to say that you have to marry me – and I know you do not want to marry anyone – least of all me."

"Are you saying that your stepmother plotted this? And I was invited to stay here at the Castle, just so that I should have to marry you?"

He was thinking the whole scenario out in his own mind as he spoke.

He was not surprised when Celina answered,

"Stepmama – is completely determined to get rid of me. When she received a letter from London – telling her that someone called Isobel wanted to marry you – she then made Papa invite you to stay here for the fishing."

The Marquis was just beginning to realise what had happened, but he managed to enquire in a very quiet tone,

"Why does your stepmother want you married?"

"She wants to be rid of me, because, as Papa does not have a son, in Scotland the title and the estate can go in the female line."

"Yes, I know that – "

"Stepmama wants Papa's money – and she thinks if I am married off to a rich aristocrat, then Papa will leave her everything which is not entailed. Meanwhile he wants his money to be spent on the estate when he is dead."

"So in fact your stepmother is determined to get rid of you. Is this her first attempt?"

Celina shook her head.

"No. She told me that I had to marry Mr. Ignatius Hambleton, who lives on the other side of the County."

"Why did you not marry him?" asked the Marquis.

He saw Celina shudder.

"She had pushed him into proposing to me, but then I had heard how – cruel he was to his horses. Then when I saw him, he was old – and repulsive. When he asked me to marry him, as Stepmama had arranged, I told him I would – rather die than be his wife!"

She spoke in a way which told the Marquis without words how horrified and terrified she had been by the man.

"So Mr. Hambleton went away, and what then did your stepmother do?"

"She beat me," whispered Celina shyly. "My back was agony for weeks."

She gave a little sob.

"When she told me – that I had to marry you – I knew I could not bear it all to happen again."

"Why did you not tell your father?"

"That is what I wanted to do," replied Celina. "But Stepmama said that if I did, she would kill both my horses and injure my arm – so that I would never be able to ride or fish again."

The Marquis's lips tightened.

He gazed at Celina as if he could scarcely believe what he had just heard.

He knew, however, it must be the truth.

He reflected that any woman who could behave in such a vile manner should be sentenced to death.

Because he was silent, Celina murmured,

"I do know that you – don't want to marry me and I don't want to marry you – but Stepmama will force Papa to tell you that you have ruined my reputation and to save it you have – to ask me to be – your wife."

The words came jerkily from her lips and now the tears were running down her cheeks.

"The whole story, Celena, is absolutely appalling, and I can only say I am extremely shocked that any woman could possibly behave in such a disgusting way."

He thought it made it worse because Celina was so small and fragile – she seemed almost lost in the big bed.

The tears running down her cheeks made her look pitiful and he was aware that her long golden hair falling over her shoulders made her very lovely.

Celina clasped her hands together.

"Please – don't be angry – with me, my Lord," she pleaded. "I know how horrible it is for you to hear all this – and when Stepmama told me tonight that I had to come in here and stay with you – I wanted to throw myself into the sea!"

She paused before she added brokenly,

"Perhaps – that is what I ought – to have done."

"It would have been extremely wicked of you," the Marquis scolded her, "and also very stupid. What we have to do, Celina, and it is going to be very difficult, is to save ourselves."

"How can we do so?"

"I am just thinking of a plan. Now tell me first how long are we meant be here before it is discovered you are sleeping in my bed?"

"I don't know exactly. But Stepmama said that I was to do anything – you wanted me to do, and if I made a fuss, she would beat me again."

The Marquis pursed his lips together.

He realised what the Countess expected to happen after she had made him drunk with her 'night cap' and the more he learnt about her, the more wicked he believed her to be.

Aloud he said quietly,

"Well, we have some time and we must be certain we are not interrupted before we can escape and I am going to lock the door now."

He rose from the bed as he spoke and he was aware that Celina shrank back as if she thought he was going to touch her.

He walked over to the door and turned the key in the lock and then, without hurrying, he returned to the bed.

"I am thinking of what we can do – "

"It is going to be very difficult for you not to marry me," Celina said slowly. "I know Stepmama will make out to Papa that – you have taken advantage of me, although I am not at all certain – what that means. She would make things extremely difficult for you if you refuse to save my reputation."

She gave a sob before she added,

"She might even write – to the Prince of Wales."

"I am not concerned about the Prince of Wales or anyone else. I am worried about *you*, Celina. You do not want to get married to a man you do not love, just as I will not marry until I am much older and in love with someone who I believe will make me a perfect wife."

"I was sure that you would think like that, but I am afraid there is nothing you can do about it – now you are in here and Stepmama – will pretend to be very angry at what has happened."

"I understand exactly what she is planning. Only a woman who is so utterly despicable could think out such a dastardly plot."

He recognised as he spoke that the Countess was in fact wreaking her revenge on him.

He had refused what she had offered him all those years ago and there is no fury like a woman scorned.

He walked over to the window and pulled back the curtains.

He could see the moonlight had turned the garden into a fairyland and in the distance he could see the lights on *The Neptune* as it was moored at the end of the jetty.

He stood gazing at his yacht.

Almost as if a message suddenly came to him, he knew what he must do.

He turned back.

"Now listen to me carefully, Celina, I want you to tell me what relatives you have on your mother's side of the family, and if there is any way we can get in touch with them."

Celina looked surprised for a moment and then she replied,

"My grandmother is alive and she has written many times to say she would love to see me. She lives near Bath because she likes to take the waters. But Papa says it is too far for him to travel with me."

"Any other relatives?"

"I have an aunt who never married and she too lives near Bath with Grandmama."

"Very well," said the Marquis. "That is where I am going to take you."

"But how can you do so, my Lord?"

"My yacht is down below at the jetty and somehow we both have to go aboard without your stepmother being aware of it."

Celina's eyes opened wide.

There was a look of excitement in them that had not been there before.

"Do you mean it? Do you *really* mean it?"

"Of course, I mean it, Celina. You do not suppose we are going to stay here and let your stepmother catch us by a wicked trick, and force us to marry when neither of us has any wish to do so."

Celina sat up even further in the bed.

"Just tell me what we are to do," she asked him in a breathless voice.

The Marquis looked at the clock.

It was now after midnight.

"Where is your stepmother's room located? Is it on this side of the Castle?"

Celina nodded.

"Yes, her room and Papa's are on the other side of the stairs. They overlook the garden and the bay – "

She saw the expression on the Marquis's face and added quickly,

"But she takes two sleeping draughts every night, because she says that Papa snores."

The Marquis smiled.

"That is exactly what I wanted to hear. Now listen, Celina, we must not make any mistakes."

"No – of course not, my Lord."

"What I want you to do is creep back to your room quietly and collect whatever clothes you need to take with you. Sensible things, because you will be at sea."

"You are taking me – on your yacht?"

"We have to reach it first. So do exactly what I tell you. Go to your room which I know is not far from here, and I think it would be best if you packed everything into a sheet rather than a box. My valet, Gilbert, will carry it for you, so you can take quite a lot of clothes. Once we are away from here we can always stop and buy anything you may have forgotten."

"Do you really believe – we can do it?"

"I don't intend to be beaten by your stepmother or to be forced into a marriage neither of us wants."

"I will go to my room at once," said Celina. "I am sure that Stepmama will not hear me in the passage."

She jumped out of the bed.

The Marquis noticed how exquisite her slim body was against the light of the candles and her nightgown was somewhat transparent.

He wondered, although he did not mention it, why her stepmother had forbidden her to bring a dressing gown with her. Nor did she have any slippers.

She walked towards the door and the Marquis saw that her golden hair hung down to her waist.

'She is very lovely and innocent,' he mused, 'and one day she will find and marry a man she loves and be really happy. I will *not* allow this cruel woman to ruin her precious life.'

Celina reached the door and he hurried to turn the key for her.

As he opened the door, he whispered,

"Dress yourself. Put everything you want to take with you on a sheet on the floor. Then I will send Gilbert to collect it in about ten minutes."

"I will be ready and thank you, thank you for being so wonderful. I never thought for a single moment – that you would save me as if you were the Archangel Gabriel."

The Marquis had opened the door and she slipped through it.

He smiled as he saw her hurrying in the direction of her bedroom.

He had been compared to many heroes in his life, but this was the first time a woman had thought of him as the Archangel Gabriel!

He waited until Celina was out of sight and then he crossed the passage to where he knew Gilbert's room was.

It was a blessing, he thought, that he did not have to climb up to the attics to find him.

He opened the door and almost immediately Gilbert called out from the bed,

"Who is it?"

The Marquis went a little nearer to him.

"I am in trouble, Gilbert, and you have to help me to escape."

Gilbert sat up.

"What's happened, my Lord?"

"They are trying to make me marry Lady Celina. So we are going to sail away in *The Neptune* before anyone finds out what we are doing."

"I'll be with your Lordship in a few minutes."

The Marquis left the room and went back into his own bedroom and as he did so he thought of one thing with a fair amount of satisfaction.

If he took Celina away as he intended to do, no one could say she was not properly chaperoned as Mrs. Gordon was on board.

Even as the idea came to him, he sat down at the writing desk that stood by the window.

Moving the candles onto it, so that he could see, he hastily scribbled a note to the Earl.

He pondered that there was nothing his wife would be able to do, but accept that she had been defeated – her appalling plot had ended in failure.

He wrote,

"My Lord,

I deeply regret to tell you that I have had an urgent message from my yacht to inform me that one of my close relatives is dangerously ill and asking to see me.

It's, of course, a plea that I cannot refuse and you must therefore forgive me for leaving immediately without saying goodbye.

Your daughter, Celina, has told me that she is very anxious to see her grandmother and this is an opportunity for her to go to London, where I will arrange for someone responsible to take her to Bath.

On my yacht she will be adequately chaperoned by Mrs. Gordon, the Captain's wife, who is travelling with me as a guest. You met her the other day when I showed you round.

Thank you many times for a few excellent days on the river. I only wish I could stay longer.

Yours affectionately,

Oliver."

He thought the Earl would find nothing suspicious in that – only the Countess would understand exactly what had happened.

He had just finished the note and was putting it into an envelope when Gilbert rushed in. He was carrying his own case and the one for his Master's clothes.

Without speaking, as if he knew it was important for them to be as quiet as possible, he started taking items out of the chest of drawers and the wardrobe.

The Marquis was ready to help, but Gilbert was so experienced there was really no need.

The Marquis glanced at the clock.

He thought that by now Celina would have laid out all she needed and she should have changed into something more substantial than what she had been wearing.

Gilbert closed the case.

"I told Lady Celina to put everything in a sheet, as I thought it might be difficult for her to find a trunk at this time of night. And I will carry what you cannot manage."

Gilbert nodded and without speaking slipped out of the room.

The Marquis looked round to see that nothing was left behind and then he put the note he had just written on his bed.

When he did not appear at breakfast time, doubtless a servant would be sent up to see what had happened.

It was only a matter of minutes before Gilbert came back, carrying a sheet full of clothes with Celina following him, holding a light bag.

The Marquis suspected she had put her hairbrushes in it and everything she needed from her dressing table.

She was dressed very sensibly in a dark gown with a shawl round her shoulders.

He guessed that she wanted to be as unobtrusive as possible – yet even in the candlelight he could see her eyes were shining like stars.

She was clearly wildly excited by their adventure.

She did not speak and the Marquis ordered Gilbert in a whisper,

"Take us downstairs where no one will see us and, of course, avoid the night-footman if he is in the hall."

"Follow me, my Lord."

Gilbert strode ahead.

The Marquis indicated for Celina to follow him and he picked up Gilbert's case, which was smaller and lighter than his own.

Gilbert led them down the servants' backstairs, then through the kitchen where there was no one to be seen, but for a couple of cats sleeping in front of the stove.

They hurried out through the kitchen door and into the garden.

It was then that Celina took over and she led them along the dark side of the garden towards the shore some distance from the jetty where *The Neptune* was moored.

There was a wide wall surrounding the garden at this point, so that they could not be seen from the windows of the Castle until they were actually half-way to the jetty.

It was then because both his arms were encumbered with carrying their clothes that Gilbert stood back.

He let the Marquis go first and he hurried down the jetty, conscious that Captain Gordon always had one of the sailors on duty at night.

To his relief, as he neared the yacht, he could see a sailor standing in the bow. He was looking at the moors with the moonlight shining on them.

Thinking it was a mistake to call out, the Marquis whistled and the second time he did so, the sailor turned round.

Then the Marquis was waving his handkerchief to attract his attention.

He came hurrying to the side of the yacht and it was only a matter of a few minutes before they were on board.

"Wake the Captain," the Marquis ordered, "and tell him I wish to put to sea immediately."

"Aye, aye, my Lord," replied the sailor.

He asked no questions and as if it was quite a usual routine, he saluted the Marquis and went below.

The powerful engines of *The Neptune* began to turn over even before Captain Gordon came up to the Saloon.

The Marquis and Celina were waiting for him there, Gilbert having gone below to the cabins with the luggage.

Captain Gordon entered.

"Good evening, my Lord. I understand you wish to put to sea."

"It is a matter of urgency, Captain, and I would be grateful if you would move out of the harbour as quietly as possible."

It was then that Celina spoke up – she had not said a word since they had left her bedroom.

"Oh, please," she implored the Marquis, "before we go to London, can we sail in your beautiful yacht and see – the Orkney Islands? I have longed to see them ever since I was a child, but something has always prevented me from going. As Papa does not have a yacht, I had almost given up hope of ever seeing them."

Just for a moment the Marquis hesitated.

Then he realised he had no wish to return quickly to London – otherwise Isobel would be waiting for him.

In fact, even if he took Celina to Bath, it would be as far as possible by sea.

He turned towards Celina with a smile.

"That is a good idea. I have always been interested in the Orkney Islands myself and this is certainly an ideal opportunity to see them."

"Oh, thank you! Thank you!" cried Celina. "It has been one of my dreams for years, but one I thought would never come true."

"But now it will, my Lady," exclaimed the Captain. "And may I suggest you retire for a good sleep before we cross what I know is a very rough piece of water before we actually reach the Islands."

"That is a most sensible suggestion, Captain," said the Marquis, "which we will both obey!"

He realised as he spoke and without being told that the Captain was just as anxious to see the Orkneys as he was himself.

They had always seemed somewhat mysterious and ethereal Islands and so few people who reached the North of Scotland troubled to go any further.

'It will be part of the adventure,' the Marquis said to himself.

When the Captain disappeared to go to the bridge, he stood watching *The Neptune* move away from Darendell Castle.

Just how on earth, he pondered to himself, could he ever have expected or imagined that he would have found himself in such an extraordinary situation?

He had merely planned to go on a quiet fishing visit to an old friend of his father's.

He wished he could see the fury on the Countess's

face tomorrow morning as once again her stepdaughter had managed to evade one of her wicked plots.

'The woman is nothing short of an evil she-devil,' the Marquis muttered to himself.

Then he was aware that Celina was standing beside him and as *The Neptune* slowly moved out of the bay and into the sea, she gave a deep sigh.

"We have done it!" she murmured. *"We have won! And now Stepmama – will not be able to reach me!"*

She spoke very softly as if speaking to herself.

Then she suddenly turned towards the Marquis and slipped her hand into his.

"Thank you, thank you, my Lord, from the bottom of my heart. How can I ever thank you enough for being so magnificent and for saving me?"

"You have saved me as well, Celina, but I think it is something we should wait to talk about tomorrow. Go to bed now and happy dreams. All your troubles are over."

He thought as he looked at her in the moonlight that no one could have looked happier or more excited.

And so beautiful.

"I am not only going to thank you," she said softly, "but also God because He heard my prayers."

Then without waiting for his reply, she turned away and disappeared below.

The Marquis stayed on deck thinking that Fate, or perhaps the God to whom Celina had prayed, had certainly saved her and him.

It had been very nearly a disaster – so close that it made him almost shudder to think about it.

He had to admit that the Countess had thought out her plot very cleverly.

There was no doubt in his mind that if he had drunk 'the nightcap' and if he had not been lucky enough to reach his yacht, everything would have been very different.

He would certainly have been trapped into walking down the aisle with Celina on his arm.

He looked up at the watery moon and smiled.

He was still a free man and he now vowed to go on fighting for that freedom.

'Nothing and no one,' he swore, 'will force me to embark on matrimony until I am ready to do so.'

CHAPTER SIX

By the time the Marquis woke in the morning, *The Neptune* had passed by Duncansby Head and was entering the Pentland Firth.

The Marquis had left it up to the Captain to choose which part of the Orkneys they were to visit first.

But he thought that he would be likely to make for Kirkwall, as it was, as far as he could remember, the most interesting and intriguing of the Orkney towns.

He went to the Saloon for breakfast and found that Celina was already there.

"It is so thrilling!" she exclaimed. "We are leaving Scotland behind and I am sure that you will be enchanted to see the Orkneys."

"I have never really thought that much about them before," admitted the Marquis. "So you will have to help me with my history."

"I have read a lot about all the Islands. That is why I am so keen to visit the Orkneys, but as I have told you, Papa does not have a yacht and it is very expensive to rent one."

"Well, now you have your wish, so you must make the best of it."

"You can be quite certain I will!"

The Marquis thought again that it suited him not to be in a hurry to return to England.

He could go to his house in the country rather than to his London house, but he was still worrying that Isobel would follow him there and try once again to make him marry her.

'The longer I stay away the better,' he determined.

He wondered if there was any good fishing in the Orkneys and perhaps he could rent a stretch on a river for a short time.

He did not mention this idea to Celina, as she might, after she had seen the Orkneys, then be longing to go to her grandmother.

In which case he would have to turn back and make for Bristol, the nearest port to Bath.

In the meantime with the charming Mrs. Gordon on board, no one could say that the girl was not chaperoned.

That was really all that mattered.

Almost as if she knew what he was thinking, Celina piped up,

"Mrs. Gordon called me this morning and she was so nice and kind. I think you are lucky to have someone so delightful on board."

"The lucky one is you, Celina, you do realise that if Mrs. Gordon had not been on board to chaperone you, your father and stepmother could so easily make the same fuss about our being on *The Neptune* as they would have made about last night at the Castle."

Celina stared at him in surprise and he realised that she had not thought of this possibility.

"But Mrs. Gordon is here," she said as if to reassure herself.

"Yes, indeed she is, and thus no one can ever claim you are unchaperoned and unprotected."

Celina gave a deep sigh of relief.

"For a moment you scared me, because I am quite sure that Stepmama will not give up easily."

"We will not think about her, Celina, and it will be best not to talk about her again. We are going to visit some magical Islands and I want you to enjoy every moment."

"I most certainly will," enthused Celina. "If they are magical Islands, it is you, my Lord, who have waved a magic wand to find a magical ship to take us there."

The way she was speaking told the Marquis that she was changing the whole venture into a fairy story.

He just knew it would be a great mistake for her to go on thinking about her stepmother.

And the same applied to him.

If this was an adventure, he wanted to forget all the difficulties that had led to it – and that included Isobel.

The sea in the Pentland Firth was always known to be rough, as it was the point where the Atlantic Ocean met the North Sea.

The Marquis told Celina she was to sit and read a book or talk to him.

"I don't want you," he said, as they sailed pass the lighthouse on Duncansby Head, "to slip up and break your leg and it is never very pleasant to be seasick!"

"I am never seasick," she boasted. "Papa and I ran into a storm once when we were in a small fishing boat and practically everyone felt sick except me."

"I still think it would be wiser to sit down!"

"And of course I will, my Lord, even though I want to see the waves splashing over the bow."

She did not argue with him which he appreciated.

"I do wish I had thought to bring one of the books from Papa's library, but I will try to remember some of the more interesting stories I have read about the Orkneys as we come to them."

She paused before she continued,

"I expect that you will know that the Islands were Scandinavian until 1468, when they came with Margaret of Denmark as part of her dowry when she married James III of Scotland and the Islanders then became far from happy with Scottish rule."

The Marquis admitted that he knew nothing about Scottish rule in the Orkneys.

"It all came to a head in 1565 and I must tell you how cruel Earl Robert Stewart, son of James V, was to the poor Islanders."

The Marquis was not particularly interested to start with, but then Celina went on to describe how by a trick, and without a sanction from the Scottish Parliament, Earl Robert had managed to acquire the Islands for himself.

Her voice was very moving as she told him about the cruelty he inflicted on their people.

"Earl Robert started off," she said, "by introducing a coinage of his own minting, and he raised the rents of the tenants to more than they could pay or endure."

"Did no one interfere to stop him, Celina?"

Celina shook her head.

"I think the truth was the Orkneys were so far away and no one worried that he gave secret encouragement to pirates who shared their booty with him."

"It seems extraordinary. Why did the authorities in Edinburgh not help the people?"

"They might have, but the Earl forbade anyone to cross over the firth without his permission. So no one in Scotland knew that he made the people build his Palaces at Kirkwall and Scalloway on the Shetlands by forced labour.

And the penalty then for dissent was torture and judicial murder."

Now the Marquis was intrigued.

He listened attentively while Celina told him how the wicked Earl had forced people to work for him without any payment.

Finally the Czar of Russia heard of this tyrant in the Islands and alerted the Earl of Caithness.

"And about time!" exclaimed the Marquis.

"It certainly was. Two great cannons were wheeled down from Edinburgh and shipped at Leith together with a strong military force."

"So the people were freed!"

"To a certain extent, but they never wholly regained their freedom and happiness until recently."

"I am very glad such horrors no longer exist."

But the Marquis then mused that there may still be local horrors around like Celina's stepmother.

'I refuse to think about her,' he told himself again, but she kept coming back into his thoughts.

*

They spent that night in a small bay on the Island of South Ronaldsay and the next morning they set off, making for Kirkwall.

Celina was so delighted by everything she saw – all the small Islands and the lighthouses thrilled her.

And as they passed places of interest on the shore, the Marquis found that she was as good as any guide.

Now that she was no longer frightened she talked to him with the same eagerness and enjoyment as she did to her father.

To the Marquis this was a new experience.

He had never in his life been alone with a lovely woman without her expecting him to flirt with her and to pay her compliments and talk endlessly about herself.

Everything Celina had to say was either about the Orkneys or the sport they were both interested in.

At times she was like an excited child – she would jump up from the table at luncheon to run on deck because there was a ship in sight.

At other times, especially at nightfall, she seemed to slip into a mysterious world all of her own.

A world, the Marquis surmised, where there would be magicians and fairies, mermaids and undoubtedly giants and hobgoblins.

She was surprisingly well read and he found that he had to polish up his history so that he could argue with her over the many wars between England and France.

"The English were horribly cruel," Celina asserted positively, "and I am *very* glad that I am a Scot!"

"I believe your mother was English?"

"Half English. My grandmother is English, which is why she likes Bath, but my grandfather was entirely of Highland blood."

She stated this so proudly that the Marquis laughed and teased her.

"Now you are being a snob. I know the Highlanders think they are superior to the Lowlanders and far superior to the English!"

"Which is what they are," Celina said aggressively.

"Very well – I am waiting for you to prove it."

"I hope I will have an opportunity," retorted Celina. "Then you will have to admit that I am right!"

She paused for a moment before she added,

"I am certainly not forgetting, my Lord, that you, an Englishman, have been wonderfully kind to me and you are exceedingly clever."

The Marquis bowed deeply.

"Thank you," he muttered sarcastically.

"No, I mean it. You not only thought of escaping yourself but of taking me with you. And I realise how very brilliant you were about it."

She did not speak in the sort of sentimental, sugar-sweet tone in which the Marquis was so used to receiving compliments.

She spoke as if she was admiring him just as a hero and simply stating the facts about him.

That as he well knew was something very different from what he was accustomed to.

As they steamed further along the East side of the Orkneys, they came to the Island of Shapinsay.

Further North there were many more Islands which the Marquis thought they might explore later on.

He kept saying to himself that there was no hurry as the longer they spent on this adventure, the easier it would be for him when he returned to England!

*

It was on the next morning that Celina asked if they could go ashore at Shapinsay.

"It is an Island noted for its flowers," she told the Marquis, "and it would be really delightful to see if it is as beautiful as it is written up to be."

He thought her suggestion was a good idea.

As the sun was shining and there was little wind, he asked the Captain to find a small quiet bay where it would be easy for them to disembark.

The Captain was only too willing to oblige as just like the Marquis, he always felt the need to explore new places.

They sailed on for a mile or more and then he drew into a small bay that was large enough for *The Neptune* to anchor in.

A boat was lowered into the water and two sailors rowed the Marquis and Celina ashore.

"I hope we have chosen a good place," said Celina. "It looks very lovely and there appear to be no cottages in sight."

"There are no towns or villages on the map I looked at," replied the Marquis, "and it will do us good to stretch our legs."

The sailors beached the boat so that they did not get their feet wet and they informed the Marquis that one of them would be on duty in *The Neptune* to receive his signal when he wished to return.

"We will not be away for too long, but bring a boat to us as soon as I signal."

"Aye, aye, my Lord."

They climbed up a low cliff and up a rough twisting path that had obviously been used many times before.

When they reached the top of the cliff, there was no sign of any human beings.

The ground was uncultivated and to Celina's great delight it was covered in a mass of wild flowers.

"We have chosen the right place," she called out to the Marquis. "I just love wild flowers and I will pick a big bouquet to take back to *The Neptune*."

"Let's go and explore the woods first," the Marquis suggested. "Although I have a feeling that we will not find anything different from what we can see now."

"There might be caves or even ruins of a Church or Castle. The books I have read say that there are plenty of these on different Islands and I would love to see one."

"We will certainly look," smiled the Marquis.

As they walked towards the nearest wood, Celina kept stopping to pick wild orchids and many other flowers she found entrancing.

"I am very glad we anchored here," she enthused. "This is a lovely Island and I am certain that some of the Islands have been spoilt not only by the outbuildings of the wicked Earl Robert, but by other Earls of the Orkneys each competing for their place in posterity."

The Marquis laughed.

"That is so true of men everywhere, not only in the Orkneys."

"I suppose you say that because you are already at the top. But there must be many people who are envious of you and who would just love to surpass you!"

The Marquis laughed again as he was thinking that she was always saying something unusual and intelligent.

Invariably he found her interesting or amusing and it suddenly struck him that for the last few days he had not been bored.

He had always imagined that if he was shut up with one woman on a ship, he would soon find her conversation monotonous and he would be utterly bored when they were not making love.

Last night he had found himself chuckling in his cabin after he had left Celina.

She had been so funny telling him about the people who had visited them in the Castle out of curiosity – and to please her father they had pretended they were sportsmen when they were not.

At other times she would talk to him about places he had visited and although she had never been lucky enough to go there herself, she had read about them.

In fact, more than once she had been able to prove him wrong on matters of history – firstly on the Rulers of Constantinople and then on the Pharaohs of Egypt.

"Celina, how can you possibly have received such a good education?" the Marquis asked.

"The Scots are very intelligent!"

"I was already aware of that before you kept telling me so!"

"Well, Papa found a good tutor for me, and I really enjoy learning. We also have an extensive library in the Castle, which I do not think you saw. I have taught myself so much about the world outside, because one day I would love to see it all."

"I hope that day will not be far away, but you will have to find a husband first."

Celina sighed.

"I suppose that it would be impossible for me to go round the world alone. But I expect if I had a husband, he would always find a good excuse for fishing or shooting at home rather than climbing the Himalayas!"

The Marquis chortled.

"Is that what you would like to do, Celina?"

"Of course, but you will just tell me scornfully that I cannot do it because I am a *woman*."

They had argued about this issue for some time.

Then the Marquis realised that he had made her tell him all about the dangers of climbing the Himalayas as she had obviously read a dozen books on the subject.

'She is certainly very unusual,' he told himself for the hundredth time as he thought over what she had said.

Now as they walked further into the wood, Celina gave a little cry.

"Look! There is a Castle in front of us."

The Marquis saw that there was indeed a Castle or rather the ruins of one.

It had once been very large and although one of its two high turrets seemed intact, the other had collapsed.

"Oh, do let's go and explore it," Celina urged him. "It is empty, but it will give us an idea of what the Orkney Castles were like. There were, I believe, a great number of them."

"We will go and take a look ," the Marquis agreed. "At the same time we must be careful. We do not want the roof falling on our heads or to be trapped in some dungeon just because you wish to explore it!"

Celina laughed.

"I am prepared to ignore the dungeons if I can see the Castle, my Lord."

They walked on through what must have been the Castle garden, but now there were only weeds and stones.

The Marquis saw that there was a doorway in front of them and made for it.

There was no glass left in the windows and the roof which must have been very spectacular in its time certainly needed repair.

But he was surprised to find the doors themselves were still standing.

When he pushed hard at one of the doors, it opened without any difficulty.

Then, as they walked in, suddenly and without any warning several men sprang at them.

As Celina screamed out, the Marquis felt a rope go round his body.

Two men bound him and although he struggled, it was too late.

His arms were tied firmly to his side and the men held him firmly and there was nothing he could do.

Another man tied a rope around Celina and she too was completely helpless.

"What does this all mean?" demanded the Marquis. "Why are you doing this?"

The men did not answer.

They only pushed him along the passage in front of them and there was nothing he could do but move between them as they compelled him to do.

He was aware that Celina was being pushed along behind him.

In a frightened voice she asked,

"What is happening? Where are they taking us?"

"I have no idea, Celina, but there is nothing we can do about it at present."

They walked on and came to a staircase and one of the men went ahead pulling the Marquis with another man behind pushing him forward.

They climbed a great number of stairs so that they were now on the second floor of the Castle, which, to the Marquis's surprise, was in a much better condition than he might have expected.

The floorboards seemed to be sound and the walls, although devoid of decoration, were intact and there were only a few holes in the ceiling overhead.

His captors now pulled him and Celina to a door at the end of a passage.

They knocked on the door and a man's voice called out to enter.

To the Marquis's surprise the room was in an even better condition than the passage outside.

In the centre of the room was a table and seated at it was a middle-aged man with dark hair and reasonably well dressed.

The men who had bound the Marquis propelled him forward until he was standing in front of the man seated at the table and a few seconds later Celina joined him.

In an untroubled voice, the Marquis spoke up,

"I think that there has been some mistake. I am the Marquis of Kexley and we were exploring what I believed was an uninhabited Island. If we have been trespassing on your property, we can only apologise."

The man sitting at the table listened to the Marquis and then he said,

"I thinks you must be an important man when I sees your ship. Well, as it 'appens, I've 'eard of you, my Lord Marquis, and I'm ever so glad to make you acquaintance."

"Now will you be kind enough to tell your men to remove these ropes around us," replied the Marquis firmly.

The man gave what seemed to Celina to be a sort of diabolical chuckle.

"Now that's a different matter altogether, and that be somethin' that us 'as to discuss."

"What can that possibly be?"

"It'll cost you a bit to go free and seein' just who you are, I'm naturally goin' to expect you'll find it easy to pay me."

"This is such extraordinary behaviour," the Marquis protested. "And I just cannot believe that this Castle really belongs to you or the land surrounding it."

The man cackled.

"I'm ain't goin' to argue with you about that. But I'm 'ere and as far as I knows no one 'as a better reason than I 'ave for possessing the Castle and the land round it."

The Marquis recognised that in his present position it would be a mistake to quarrel with him.

"I have already apologised for intruding onto your land, and if you want to be paid for any damage I may have done, I will naturally do so."

"Now that be the right way to talk, my Lord, and what I wants to 'ear. I should think seein' as who you are and the size of your ship that ten thousand pounds will not be too difficult for you to find, and it's what I needs badly at the moment."

"*Ten thousand pounds*!" cried the Marquis. "You have to be joking!"

"It's no joke," their captor responded. "Either you pays up or you stays until you does."

"You cannot expect me to have that sum of money on me or on my yacht," the Marquis said loftily.

"Well, I'll take a cheque, and with your name I'll cash it in Kirkwall. Maybe it'd be wise to take the Captain of your ship along with us to make sure the bank won't fail to recognise who you be."

"I am prepared to give you a reasonable amount of money," the Marquis suggested, playing for time. "But ten thousand pounds is far too much and the bank would most certainly want a great deal of assurance before parting with such a sum."

"I'll convince them it ain't no trick, and as they've dealt with me a few times afore, they knows only too well what'll 'appen if them don't pay up."

The Marquis realised that this man had obviously used force to intimidate the bank and he strongly suspected that he had a great many more followers than the three men they had already seen.

He guessed that he might be one of the infamous pirates who still operated round the North of Scotland and the Orkneys.

The British Navy had attempted to control them for many years, but the Marquis remembered reading that they could sneak in from Norway and Sweden.

They were past masters at handling the light quick sailing boats they frequently used and they knew every bay and cave where they could hide out.

"I think that you must give me time to discuss this with the lady," the Marquis continued, "and naturally I am not carrying a cheque book with me."

As if the man facing him became aware of Celina for the first time, he turned his head to look at her.

Then it was obvious that he was surprised.

In her struggles with the man when he first put the rope around her, the shady hat she was wearing had fallen off her head.

The sun coming through the window glinted on the gold of her hair and although she was clearly terrified, she still looked very beautiful.

The Marquis was fully aware of the way she was being scrutinised by the pirate – if that was what the ruffian indeed was.

He said quickly,

"Because I do not wish my wife to be frightened or bound in the way she is now, I suggest you set us both free. I will go straight to the yacht to get you at least some of the money you request."

He noticed, as he referred to Celina as his wife, that she looked at him in surprise and then looked away again.

"You send first for your chequebook and then us'll talk business. You might find it quite comfortable where I be puttin' you, but it ain't the luxury you're accustomed to, nor can I provide you with any food or drink."

Then sitting up in his chair, he gave orders sharply to the three men who had bound them.

He spoke now in a different language.

The Marquis was uncertain at what was being said, but he thought he recognised the word 'turret'.

Without his being able to say anything further, the men pulled Celina and him out of the room.

They were dragged up a winding staircase that he had not noticed earlier, and as they began to climb and the stairs twisted, the Marquis realised they were in a turret.

It was the turret that he and Celina had noticed was not as damaged as the others.

They climbed up for a long time until their captors were breathing heavily and even the Marquis was finding it hard work.

There was a door ahead and he felt that they must be at the top of the turret and when the men pushed him and Celina through it, he could see that they were now in a round room with a low ceiling.

They had not quite reached the top and it was then he remembered the turret they had seen from the ground rose to a high tapered point.

According to Celina this was very characteristic of Orkney Castles.

The room was furnished sparsely with a table, two chairs and a rickety iron bedstead.

The men unwound the ropes they had put round the Marquis and Celina.

"How long will we have to stay here?" the Marquis asked them.

They did not answer and he then realised that they did not understand him.

The chief pirate had spoken to them in a language that might have been that of the Orkney Islanders or some Scandinavian tongue.

Without saying anything the men went out through the door and the Marquis heard them lock it firmly behind them and there was a clatter of their footsteps going below.

Celina looked round and gave a little cry.

"Just how could this have happened to us? It was all my fault for wanting to explore the Castle."

"But how could either of us have imagined that this could have befallen us?" replied the Marquis gently.

He walked over to a small window with bars across it and he could see the wood they had walked through.

"What is going to happen to us?" Celina asked.

"I think the man in charge will go to the yacht and ask for my chequebook. It will be difficult for the Captain to refuse him, but he may be sensible enough to send two sailors with it."

"And we have to stay here – until they return?"

"I cannot see any way of getting out," the Marquis admitted. "The windows are too small and, as you can see, heavily barred, while the door is securely locked."

"But you cannot give them as much as ten thousand pounds – it is a fortune!"

"What I really resent, Celina, is being so weak that I could not resist them taking us prisoner."

He sat down in the chair and put his fingers up to his forehead.

"We have escaped once in a very astute way," he said, "and now we have to think of another one."

Celina walked over to the door and felt the lock – if everything else was old and dilapidated in the Castle, the lock had obviously been added recently.

The Marquis suspected that the pirates were making a fortune out of kidnapping tourists and extracting money from them.

He had to concede that what he had been asked for was a very large sum and he suspected that ordinary people were forced into paying up whatever they had on them – perhaps only a few pounds.

Now he thought it over he remembered hearing that there were pirates and thieves of every sort in some of the Orkney Islands.

The Captain had actually mentioned earlier it would be a mistake to let anyone come aboard as sightseers.

"I've heard in these parts they are not too particular as to who owns what," the Captain had said. "And I've no wish to lose anything from *The Neptune*."

"I do agree with you," the Marquis had commented. "And please see that there are arms available for the crew, if we are unfortunate enough to need them."

He had not repeated this conversation to Celina as he had thought it would scare her, but he wished now that he had been sensible enough to bring his revolver with him when he came ashore.

Celina turned from the door,

"You cannot pay all that money, it is *wicked*. That horrible man will only spend it on riotous living, while you can do so much good with it."

"I agree with you, Celina, so what we must do now is try to escape, but I cannot see any possible way of doing so as long as we are locked up in this turret."

Celina looked around and then she tipped back her head to have a good look at the ceiling.

"Just look at that!" she exclaimed pointing upwards with her finger.

The Marquis looked up too and saw that there was a trapdoor in the ceiling and it did not look as if it had been used for many years.

The ceiling itself was rough and most of the plaster had fallen off so that the bare boarding was revealed.

"Are you suggesting that we climb up to it?"

Celina shook her head.

"I am just thinking that it must have been used for a certain purpose on the part of the evil Earl Robert."

The Marquis thought that there was no way it could help them escape.

"If you are thinking it might help us in some way, I will stand on the table and try to open it from here."

"Yes, do try, but don't hurt yourself."

The trapdoor was almost directly over the table at which the Marquis was sitting and he climbed onto it.

Then putting his hand on the centre of the trapdoor, he pushed.

There was no reaction at all.

In fact, as far as he was concerned, he might have been pushing solid iron.

"I thought that would happen," sighed Celina. "It has to be opened from above."

The Marquis looked down at her from the table.

"How do you suggest we do that?"

To his surprise Celina then walked over to one of the windows – there were four in the turret and they were all without glass.

It did strike the Marquis that it might be very cold at night and although the bed had a rough mattress on it, there were no blankets they could cover themselves with.

He climbed down from the table and was just about to repeat his question as to how they could get the trapdoor open, when there was the sound of footsteps coming up the stairs.

They both stiffened.

The key turned in the lock and the door opened.

It was the pirate who stood there with his two men beside him.

He walked to the table and slapped a piece of paper down on it and a man from behind him set beside it a small bottle of ink and a quill pen.

"Now write!" the pirate ordered. "Tell the Captain of your ship to send your chequebook and if you 'as any money on you, I'll take that now."

"I suppose there is no way that I can give you this cheque after my wife and I have returned to my yacht?" the Marquis asked him hopefully.

The pirate laughed inanely.

"You must think I'm a ninny to fall for somethin' like that. I weren't born yesterday and if you was workin' with me, I'd soon find meself clapped in irons!"

The Marquis had to admit this sounded reasonable.

"Very well," he said, "I'll send for my chequebook, but I very much doubt if the Captain will hand it over to your man."

"I've thought of that, and I shan't be sendin' until tomorrow morning. They'll be real worried about you by then and you'll be worryin' about your empty stomach!"

The way he spoke was most unpleasant and Celina gave a little cry.

131

The Marquis sat down at the table.

"Very well – have it *your* way."

It was not easy with the quill pen, but he managed to write to Captain Gordon,

"Dear Captain,

Please give this man my chequebook.

Kexley."

The pirate snatched it from him as soon as it was dry and with some difficulty he read the message.

"There is nothing on it to indicate where I am and I can only hope the Captain will give you what you require."

"If he don't," the pirate smirked, "you can write 'im another pleadin' note. He'll know that 'e won't get 'is own pay till you get back."

He put the note into his pocket and walked towards the door.

The man with him picked up the pen and ink before he followed and the door was slammed shut and locked.

They heard footsteps going slowly but noisily down the stairs.

The Marquis turned towards Celina – she had stood by the window without moving all the time the pirates had been in the room.

Now she ran towards him and he thought that she was coming to him for protection and comfort.

Then when she reached him, she began to whisper and he knew this was the reason why she had come so near to him.

"I have thought of a way," she murmured, "how we can escape."

CHAPTER SEVEN

The Marquis gazed at Celina in surprise.

"How?" he asked, intrigued.

She glanced over her shoulder as if she was afraid that someone might be listening.

Then as she was reassured, she began,

"I read in the book about Earl Robert that he cut off the heads of those who had opposed him in one of these towers."

The Marquis was listening intently because she was speaking so softly.

"He would say mockingly that he executed them at the top of the Castle so they could be nearer to the Heaven they were praying to. Then the towers had the tapering pointed top just like this one."

The Marquis nodded and she went on,

"The wicked Earl soon discovered that there was very little room in the top. Only himself and no more than two of his followers could watch the execution."

"So what did he do?"

The Marquis could not understand how this could help in any way, but he was willing to listen to Celina.

"The Earl had a trapdoor built like the one you see over your head and the man to be executed was taken up above with the executioner and maybe two others. Then the Earl and his men would sit below listening to the whole grizzly proceedings."

The Marquis looked at her in surprise.

"How do you know all this?"

"I read it in a book, but I have just remembered that is why there is a trapdoor in the centre of the turret."

The Marquis looked up at it.

"But we cannot open it, if indeed you are planning to escape that way."

"I am quite certain it is fastened down from above, so I will climb up and release it. Then we can get away by going down the stairs we came up."

The Marquis stared at her.

"How on earth can you manage it?"

Celina gave a little laugh.

"I am going to climb up."

"*Outside!*" exclaimed the Marquis.

"Of course."

"Then I absolutely forbid it, Celina. If you fall, you will kill yourself or at least be injured for life."

"I have climbed up all the towers at home. I had a cousin who stayed with us two years ago and we used to race each other to see who could reach the top of the tower first."

"I still say it is far too dangerous and in any case I doubt if you could even climb out of the window."

He looked at the windows and noted again that they were all covered with two solid vertical iron bars.

Then Celina pointed with her finger and he saw that the one furthest away from them had only one bar over it – the other one must have been knocked off at some time or another.

The Marquis walked towards it.

"The only one, who will climb onto the roof of this turret, will be me."

Celina laughed.

"You are far too big, my Lord, to get through that window!"

The Marquis could see that this was true.

"Then we will just have to stay here," he persisted.

"That would be an extremely silly thing to do if it is at all possible for us to escape."

"It may cost me money and I imagine that the pirate will keep his word and let us out when he has ten thousand pounds in his grubby hands."

"You cannot be at all certain," whispered Celina. "Most of the pirates in Earl Robert's day killed their victims so that they could not give evidence against them."

The Marquis drew in his breath as he began to think that the situation was even worse than it had appeared to be at first.

Without saying anything, he moved closer to the window and looked outside and then he glanced up.

He had been about to say to Celina that even if she could reach the top of the tower, she might not be able to climb inside.

Now he saw that there were several large holes on the slanting roof of the tower and he remembered that the similar pointed tower at the other end of the Castle had collapsed altogether.

Celina was close behind him.

"We must wait until it is nearly dark, so that I will not be seen. Then I will try to open the trapdoor and you can join me."

"I am sure it is too dangerous – "

At the same time he was weakening.

It was not a long climb and he realised that it was the one and only way they could escape from the pirates.

Celina pulled on his arm.

"Come away, my Lord, just in case anyone sees us looking out and guesses what we are planning to do."

"I have not agreed to your wild scheme yet, Celina, and it scares me to even think of you taking such a risk."

"I do promise you I am a very good climber. That is why I want to visit the Himalayas."

"If you fall trying to climb this tower, there will be no question of you going anywhere!"

"I know that, but I am not afraid. Not half as afraid as I was of you!"

The Marquis smiled at her.

"Well, I am so glad that you realise I am not such a monster as that pirate!"

"He is a horrible man, and I am quite certain that if you give him the money he has demanded, he will ask for more or just kill us so that he can go on extorting money from other people."

They sat in silence for a little while.

The Marquis, despite himself, could not but think that if they really could escape, it would be very stupid to sit meekly where they were until tomorrow.

As if Celina knew instinctively he was changing his mind, she added,

"We will be very hungry and thirsty if we stay here until breakfast. What is the time now?"

The Marquis looked at his watch.

"Almost six o'clock."

"Then it will be getting dark at about eight o'clock and the pirates should be eating at that time."

"I still think it is far too dangerous, Celina, and if it was at all possible I would do it myself."

"I don't want to seem conceited, my Lord, but I am certain that I am a better climber than you are. If you have climbed, as I expect you have, it has been in the orthodox way with guides and ropes and then you were not likely to put a foot wrong.

"I have learnt to climb by sheer commonsense and because I wanted to prove that I was better than my cousin, and of course I was."

The Marquis grinned.

"I have never known a woman to be so proud of her ability to climb, especially such a rock face as a turret with a pinnacle top!"

"I always thought the mountains around Darendell were rather feeble, and actually I have been to the top of each one of them."

The Marquis gave a deep sigh.

"Very well, Celina, you win. I will allow you to do something that I feel is extremely dangerous, but I cannot think of any appropriate alternative."

"I thought you would see sense, my Lord. Now I am just going to take a quick peep at the way I shall go and I only hope there is no one watching."

"I think it is a bit unlikely, but let me look out as I am sure my eyes are sharper than yours."

"I will allow you that one superiority!" she laughed.

The Marquis now approached the window with the broken bar.

He looked out onto the ground below and over the

trees to the sea and he was prepared to swear that there was not a living soul in sight.

Then he turned away from the window without any comment and Celina took his place.

She did not waste her time glancing down from the window, but looked up and the Marquis knew that she was working out where she should place her feet and what she could cling on to for support.

It was actually only a relatively short climb, but it could be fatal for anyone who fell, especially as the ground beneath the Castle was covered with broken stones.

She came back and sat down beside the Marquis.

"It's going to seem a long wait until it begins to get dark. What shall we talk about?"

"Suppose you tell me something about yourself. I am most interested to know why you are so different from most girls of your age."

Celina giggled.

"I thought I had told you that I was brought up like a boy, and one day I hope I will be able to show you that I am a very good shot!"

"I don't approve of women shooting," the Marquis retorted quickly.

Celina giggled again.

"I was certain you would say that. I went shooting with Papa because he wanted me as a companion, but quite frankly I don't really like killing anything."

"That at least is feminine – "

"Oh, I am very feminine in some ways, and I adore children. I hope one day to have a very large family of my own."

"But you will need a husband first."

"I suppose that's a necessity, but I promise you that it will *never* be someone of Stepmama's choice."

The Marquis put up his hand.

"You are not to think about her, not at this moment at any rate."

"You are quite right, my Lord, as if I fall and kill myself, she would be positively delighted – "

"Then make absolutely sure, Celina, that we leave her regretting that you are still alive a long time after she is long gone."

There was a pause in the conversation for a moment and then Celina muttered in a very small voice,

"But I suppose I will have to go home one day – "

"I am quite certain that will be unnecessary as long as your grandmother is alive, and as you are so beautiful, Celina, a great many wonderful things might happen to you whilst you are living with her in Bath."

"Of course you are right, and I am looking forward to staying there with Grandmama."

She hesitated and then added,

"So please – let us see all of the Orkneys before we have to leave them."

"You still want to go on touring round the Islands even after what has happened to us today?"

"It is all an adventure we will be able to put in our autobiographies when we write them, and I am sure if you include photographs in yours, they will be of many, many beautiful women."

"Now you have been listening to gossip about me!"

Celina started teasing him about his reputation and she made it sound so amusing that they were both laughing almost helplessly.

It seemed as if the time had swept by before Celina remarked,

"It's getting dark. The shadows are long under the trees and the sun is sinking."

The Marquis walked to the window.

"Are you really determined to do this?" he asked.

Celina nodded vigorously and said a little coyly,

"You realise I cannot do it in my petticoats."

"I had not thought of that, but they would certainly increase your difficulties."

"If you will please not look, my Lord, I will put my clothes on the table and when I open the trapdoor, you can hand them up to me before you come up yourself."

The Marquis walked to the other side of the tower.

"I am not looking – Celina."

He heard some swift movements as she took off her shoes and her dress and he thought most of what she might be wearing underneath it as well.

"Don't look round, just pray I will be successful."

"You don't want me to help you?"

"I can manage," replied Celina, "and may God take good care of you."

He heard her movements as she squeezed through the narrow window.

Only then did he turn round and walk cautiously to the other side of the tower.

He knew that he must not startle or upset her in any way, but, as he was aware of the incredibly dangerous task she had undertaken, he was tensed up in a way that felt extremely painful.

Then he was praying as she had asked him to do.

He was begging God to take extra care of her – and that she would not fall and kill herself.

After a tortured moment, he thought it safe to look through the window and, as he did so, he saw her bare feet disappearing through a hole in the roof above them.

He felt himself relax a little.

He realised then that he had never been so afraid for anyone in his whole life as he had been for Celina.

Now he could hear her faint movements overhead.

He put up his hand to his forehead – it was damp from the intense feelings she had evoked in him.

He now guessed she was working on the trapdoor.

Almost as if he could read her thoughts, he climbed onto the table and began to push at the trapdoor with all his strength.

Suddenly it moved and went backwards with a loud bang and the noise made the Marquis start in case it could be heard from below.

Then he saw Celina's face looking down at him.

"We've done it! *We've done it,*" she whispered.

The Marquis bent down to pick up her clothes and handed them to her, as he became aware that she must have been wearing very little when she climbed up the roof.

"Give me a few minutes," she murmured.

He smiled, wondering how many other women of his acquaintance would be so modest.

But he recognised that as Celina was so young and innocent, he must be very careful not to shock her in any way.

He pulled one of the chairs onto the table, as when she was ready, it would make it easier for him to join her.

She did not take too long in dressing.

"You can come up now, my Lord," she called out.

He stood on the chair and then with no difficulty at all he pulled himself through the opening.

The top of the tower was, just as he expected, much smaller than the room below.

The roof was shattered so there would have been no difficulty for Celina in entering it once she had reached the top of the turret.

As he stepped onto the floor, Celina was standing looking at him.

Without thinking what he was doing and because he had been so desperately anxious about her, he pulled her into his arms.

His lips came down on hers.

For a moment she seemed to stiffen a little.

Then the kiss he had meant to be so gentle became very much more demanding.

For what seemed like a long time they were joined together.

The Marquis was aware that it was not merely a kiss of relief and congratulations, but it was something very different.

As he set Celina free, she slipped her hand into his and drew him towards the door.

It struck the Marquis for the first time that perhaps the door might be locked – in which case all they had done would have been useless.

To his relief it was not locked and they both walked cautiously through it into the passage.

The stairs were in darkness and, still holding Celina by the hand, the Marquis started to inch down them very very slowly.

It was essential, he knew, that they should make no noise.

In addition he was banking on Celina's suggestion that the pirates would be eating at this time of the night.

It seemed to him a long way down to the last step.

They paused for some minutes before they reached the ground and both the Marquis and Celina listened.

Then suddenly they heard a man's laugh, but it was some distance away and next another man spoke, although they could not hear what he said.

It was quite obvious that the pirates were together in a room in the Castle, but it was actually a little distance from the turret.

The Marquis remembered the door where they had entered the Castle and so holding Celina's hand, he walked very quietly towards it and opened it gently.

To his relief, he could see several low bushes just outside, so they slipped behind them.

He had already thought it would be a great mistake to cross directly to *The Neptune* the way they had come, as there was nothing to give them cover growing on the rough ground in front of the Castle.

They could easily be seen by anyone looking out of the Castle, so he deliberately turned to the left behind the bushes – then straight down a deep drop in the land and up again on the other side.

Now they were much nearer to the woods and the Marquis considered that it would be very unlikely for them to be seen as it was now almost completely dark.

The sun had disappeared and the moon had not yet risen.

The shadows were deep and once they were safely in the wood the Marquis knew that they were out of danger.

However, it would be very stupid to take any risks as there was just a chance the pirates might think of giving them something to eat or even just check up on them.

They were now well to the North of *The Neptune*, but the Marquis did not hurry down to the cliff edge.

Instead he kept among the trees until they were as near as possible to the small bay where *The Neptune* was anchored.

Still he and Celina walked on and then at last, with the woods between them and the Castle, he stopped.

Now it was just about possible to see the top of the yacht's mast.

It was then that he let go of Celina's hand and drew a deep breath.

"We have done it!"

They were the first words he had spoken since they left the turret.

"I was praying," Celina mumbled, "that they would not follow us."

"Your prayers were answered, Celina, and now we are going to sail away and forget what has happened today and it is all due to *you* that we can do so."

"And you," she whispered.

The Marquis put his arms around her and drew her close to him.

"No one could have been more marvellous."

Then he kissed Celina again.

Now he was aware that her lips were very soft and sweet beneath his.

Her arms went round his neck and he could feel her trembling.

He went on kissing her.

At first gently, then demandingly.

He became acutely conscious as he did so that his whole body was filled with a rapture he had never known before.

It was not just the fierce fire he had so often felt for other women.

It was something more perfect and ethereal and in a way almost sacred.

He could not explain it to himself.

He only knew that the feeling Celina had aroused in him was something different.

Something inexplicably wonderful.

Only when they were both breathless did he release her.

Taking Celina's hand he walked to the edge of the cliff and, as he had expected, the boat was on the beach and with it were two sailors.

Followed by Celina, he walked very carefully down the cliff path.

The sailors leapt out of their boat and were standing waiting for them when they reached it.

"We was wondering what'd happened to you, my Lord," one of them piped up. "The Captain were thinking of sending some of us over to see if your Lordship was in any trouble."

"We have indeed been in a great deal of trouble," replied the Marquis, "but you will hear about it later. All her Ladyship and I want now is to go back on board as fast as we possibly can."

He lifted Celina into the boat and as they sat side by side, the sailors rowed them out to *The Neptune*.

When they climbed aboard the Captain was waiting for them.

"Whatever happened to your Lordship?" he asked. "I was very worried as you have been away for so long."

"I was pretty worried myself, Captain, but we will tell you about it later. All you must do now is move away immediately and quietly. There are pirates on shore, but I am not sure how many there are or what danger they can still be to us."

The Captain did not waste any more time and he hurried away to the bridge.

Celina ran below as the Marquis stopped to give the Steward instructions to have dinner ready as quickly as the chef could manage.

Then he went to his own cabin where Gilbert was waiting.

"Your Lordship's given us all a bit of a turn here," he cried. "We was wondering what had happened."

As the Marquis changed into his evening clothes he told Gilbert what they had been through.

"Well, all I can say, my Lord, her Ladyship should receive a medal for what she's done. Them pirates can be really nasty I hears, if they don't get what they wants."

"That is just what I was afraid of, Gilbert."

*

The Neptune was well under way by the time the Marquis had changed.

He went onto the bridge to have a few words with Captain Gordon and then he joined Celina in the Saloon.

She was looking, he thought, very lovely in a pretty dark blue evening gown.

When their eyes met, it was impossible for him to look away.

For a moment there was nothing to say.

It was the Head Steward who broke the spell.

"Dinner is ready, my Lord. I hope you enjoy it."

He and Celina sat down and the Stewards hurried in with the first course.

There was champagne which the Marquis said they not only needed but richly deserved.

They were both hungry and still feeling the effects of shock from all they had been through.

Therefore they hardly spoke during the meal.

Only when the Stewards had gone and the Marquis had insisted on their both drinking a liqueur did he say,

"Now, my darling, we can talk about ourselves."

Celina's blue eyes widened and she blushed deeply at his endearment.

In a very soft voice she murmured,

"We are safe and that is all that matters."

"There is no one to thank except you and I find it difficult to put what I feel into words."

She knew from the way he spoke he was thinking once again of kissing her.

Again she blushed and it made her look even more exquisite than before.

Then the Marquis said very quietly,

"How soon, my precious one, will you marry me?"

Celina stared at him in astonishment.

It had never occurred to her that he would say such a thing.

The Marquis waited.

"But," Celina now hesitated, "you have no wish to – marry anyone."

"I have no wish to marry anyone but *you*. I knew when I was praying you would not fall to the ground, that if you did do so, I would lose something so precious and so perfect and that it was someone I could never find again."

Celina drew in her breath.

"I love you," she sighed, "but I *cannot* marry you."

The Marquis stared almost as if someone had struck him an unexpected blow.

He had been pursued by so many women and had been forced to run away from Isobel to escape being forced into marrying her.

It had never occurred to him that anyone he asked to marry him would refuse.

"I don't understand, Celina, I thought when I kissed you, you would realise, as I did, that you love me as much as I love you."

"I *do* love you, but so much – I cannot marry you."

"Why! Why!" the Marquis demanded.

She looked down a little shyly and as he waited she suddenly looked up again.

He could see love in her eyes.

"You do love me," he cried out, distraught. "Then *why*, my darling, will you not marry me?"

There was silence as if she was choosing her words carefully.

"Because I love you *too much*. If I did marry you and you became bored with me as you have been with so many others, it would be like being shut out of Heaven and I could never bear it."

The Marquis smiled and put his hand over hers.

"I know just what you are saying and I understand. But what I am feeling for you, my precious one, is entirely different from what I have ever felt before and that I swear on the Bible is the truth."

Celina did not reply and he continued,

"I know exactly what I really want. It is to live in the country with you and I hope one day with our children. We will devote ourselves to my estate, and concentrate on our horses and all the other sports. Together we will be as happy as I have been these last few days."

Still Celina did not say anything, but he sensed that she was listening and he carried on,

"I have never been with a woman before who made me so absorbed by a thousand different interests, which I have never connected with women, only with men."

He smiled as he added,

"We will climb the Himalayas together, my darling. Not only actually but metaphorically as well, because we both understand our respective urges to reach the top."

"And you really think that I will be enough to keep you – happy?" Celina asked him in a small voice.

"I will be miserably unhappy without you, Celina."

"But you may think I have trapped you – "

"*I am trapped*, but not by you, my adorable one – "

Celina looked at him, not quite understanding, and he said quietly,

"*By love.* A love so totally perfect, so glorious, so Divine, it can only have come from Heaven."

Celina gave a little cry.

"How can you possibly say anything so wonderful? It is something I thought I would never hear you say."

"I love you, I love you, I love you, Celina, and that is why, my exquisite one, I suggest that instead of going back to your family and mine, who will be busy telling us what to do and telling you how difficult it will be to keep me faithful, we get married at once!"

"*At once*! Do you mean here in Orkney?"

"Why ever not? There is, I believe, a magnificent Cathedral in Kirkwall and that means a Bishop, who I am sure will be only too pleased to marry us."

Celina gave a little laugh.

"That will be exciting and romantic – but you must promise to buy me a wedding dress."

"I am sure that we can find one somewhere in the town, but you look adorable and ethereally beautiful, my darling, whatever you wear – or do not wear – "

Celina blushed.

"You did *not* look when I was climbing the turret?"

"Because I knew you did not want me to, I did not. At the same time that ghastly agony of fear I went through, I hope I will never have to suffer again."

"There cannot be pirates everywhere and it will be lovely to spend our honeymoon among the Islands."

"We will," the Marquis assured her. "Equally the crew will be armed and will watch over us. I am not taking any more chances where you are concerned."

Celina slipped her hand into his.

"You are quite certain," she asked earnestly, "that you will be content with me? You have achieved so much that it is going to be difficult to keep up with you."

"But, as you think so quickly with your clever little brain, I rather suspect that you are some miles ahead of me all of the time!"

Then they were both laughing as the Marquis drew her out on to the deck.

Now the moon was shining and the stars glittered brightly above.

He thought that the Captain would now be making for North Ronaldsay, where he could anchor safely without being worried.

At the moment all he could think of was that Celina was standing beside him.

With the moonlight glittering on her hair she was like the stars themselves.

"I love you, adore you and worship you, my Celina. I love you so much that you will be bored with hearing me say it over and over again."

"And I love you," she sighed. "I knew at once when I saw you fishing that you were the most wonderful man I could ever have imagined. But I wanted to run away from you because I thought you would be angry when you learnt what Stepmama was planning."

"I think really, maybe we should both be grateful to her," the Marquis suggested surprisingly.

"*Grateful?*" exclaimed Celina.

"If she had not plotted in such a disgraceful way to force me into marrying you, it might have taken very much longer to make me realise how adorable you are and how much I want you for ever in my life."

Celina gave a little laugh.

"You are making everything seem so different."

"One thing that is not different, my darling Celina, is that I love you. And I am falling more and more in love with you every second we are together. How can you be so unique, the perfect wife I thought I would never find?"

"I want you to keep on loving me and I will try and be perfect for you, because you are the most wonderful and handsome man in the whole wide world."

There was nothing the Marquis could do after that but kiss her.

As he felt her melting into his arms, he knew how amazingly lucky he had been.

He had run away from marriage all his life.

Only because at the back of his mind he desperately wished for the ideal woman he had never found until now.

He knew that as Celina was so young and innocent, he must be very gentle with her.

At the same time he knew that her love for him was so perfect and so spiritual that it would keep them bound together for as long as they lived and beyond.

He kissed her passionately and fervently and went on kissing her.

He knew that they had found the Heaven that God has created only for lovers who truly love each other.

A very special Heaven where there was never any question of losing each other.

Only growing closer and closer until they were not two people but one in this life and for all Eternity.